D1381487

DOTTY
and the Dream Catchers

Emma Warner-Reed

First published by Calendar House Press 2017

Copyright © 2017 Emma Warner-Reed

www.thedottyseries.com

All rights reserved.

No part of this publication may be reproduced or transmitted or utilized in any form or by any means, mechanical, photocopying or otherwise without the prior permission of the publisher.

Cover design by Emma Warner-Reed

Designed and Typeset by Emma Warner-Reed

The DOTTY Series Vol. 3 – DOTTY and the Dream Catchers

Summary:

It's all change for Dotty, as Great-Uncle Winchester decides it's high time she went to school. But the transition back into school life isn't easy: Dotty is being haunted by disturbing dreams. What is more, a mystery illness is taking over the school. Dotty's classmates are convinced she has something to do with it, and Dotty isn't entirely sure they're wrong. Is there more to Dotty's dreams than meets the eye? And can a little bit of sweeps' magic save the day?

ISBN:978-0-9955662-6-2

What people have to say about DOTTY:

"Author Emma Warner-Reed has penned a magnificent children's book with suspense that builds as young readers are drawn into the mystery surrounding Dotty's new home. Dotty and the Calendar House Key is highly recommended for home and school libraries and has earned the Literary Classics Seal of Approval."

Literary Classics Book Reviews
Amazon

"Dotty and the Calendar House Key has truly fired my daughter's imagination for the first time since Harry Potter. Beautifully written and exciting. The Secret Garden meets Diagon Alley. Fabulous!"

A Vere
Harrogate

"My son has just read the first [book] and thinks it's brilliant - high praise since he has very decided opinions about what he reads."

P Uglow
Harrogate

"I really liked the [first] book. It was a bit scary when Dotty found herself in Uncle Winchester's private study. But most of the books I read are a bit scary so that was okay. I would read the other books in the series. Go Team Dotty!"

Betty, age 7
Amazon

"Enchanting, innocent and lovely with just the right amount of modern technology...a great read for a grown up 7 year old! She loved it... When is the next one coming out?"

A Little
Amazon

"What a thoroughly enjoyable read this series is turning out to be. The Calendar House world is definitely a place worth visiting and revisiting. Dotty the perfect protagonist with more than two dimensions to her character is sassy, brave and very curious. Children will wallow in the luxurious imagery created by Emma Warner-Reed."

P D Lovell
Switzerland

"Dotty takes you yet again on a truly fantastic fascinating fantasy adventure, meeting even more amazing magical characters. Well done Emma - we love your imagination: chimneys have become more than just chimneys in this house since Dotty's first adventure. What a wonderful series this is turning out to be, When is the film coming out?"

R Libera
North Yorkshire

For further information and updates on The DOTTY Series visit:

www.thedottyseries.com

To anyone who is chasing their dreams
– I hope you catch them.

CONTENTS

Contents

Prologue

Fight and Flight

"You fool!" The Vagabond King's rage exploded into every corner of the small dark cellar room. Cower as he might, his henchman could not escape it. Mordecai shrank back into the wall, but the imposing figure of the King loomed over the trembling bird, engulfing him in shadow.

Mordecai scraped and bowed. His mechanical eye whirred and clicked, its lens moving backwards and forwards erratically, the camera's frantic motion betraying his inner turmoil. "I thought ye would be pleased, Master. The treasure be worth far more than the small trinket I exchanged for it."

"Worth more?" thundered the King. "Worth more, you say?" He swept his arm across the table, the sleeve of his patched woollen greatcoat scattering gold pieces and multi-coloured gems across the room in every direction. "The Calendar House Key, that 'trinket' as you call it, is worth a thousand piles of this precious treasure of yours." The King paced up and down the room in a fury, his heavy-booted strides shaking the very walls. "Did it not occur to you that the Key might hold some special importance to me, given the lengths to which we went to procure it?

"Tell me, what use is gold to us?" he continued to rant. "Can it close chimneys? Can it prevent the ignorant folk of the ordinary world from chimney travel? No, it cannot." He brought his fist down hard on the wooden table. "But taking the Calendar House Key from them can."

"If only I had known, Master." The bird simpered.

"It is not your place to know, Mordecai. It is your place to obey," stormed the King. "And when I think that you bargained it away, that you were fooled into trading something of such value—to the hob, of all creatures—well, it makes me want to weep. It is because of your carelessness that we have not only lost the hob, now we have lost the Key as well. And all for what: a single pot of gold?"

"It was a very large pot," the bird retorted, ruffling his feathers indignantly. "And anyway, the hob's escape was not my doing. I warned ye not to leave it alone with the boy. Faeries be tricksy, I said."

"Dare you to challenge me?" The King swooped forward, grabbing hold of the bird by its mechanical eye.

Mordecai squawked and squirmed, trying to evade his master's grasp, but to no avail.

"This is the problem," said the King, "this eye. It was supposed to bring me information, not show you glittering objects to covet. I should have known never to trust a greedy magpie." And with an iron grip the Vagabond King ripped the eye clean from the magpie's head.

"Give it back to me! Give it back," Mordecai squawked blindly, hopping from one clawed foot to the other, snapping his beak wildly about him.

"Give you this?" the King mocked viciously, holding the mechanical eye up high above the bird's head as he danced about below it. "When this has been the cause of all my misery? I'm warning you, we had better find a way to get the locket back, Mordecai the Eyeless, or you and I are through."

Then with one final swish of his greatcoat, the Vagabond King stepped into the chimney and disappeared, taking the source of his henchman's vision with him and leaving the sightless bird shrieking and wailing away into the night.

Fight and Flight

Chapter 1

Sarah

"Sarah, slow down! I can't keep up."

Once again Dotty found herself trapped in the same strange vision she had been having for months now. It was almost becoming a nightly routine: waking the moment after sleep claimed her. Finding herself, not in her bed, but in a forest, and there was no way she could have got to wherever it was so fast, or in her pyjamas. At least she thought not.

Tonight was no different, and Dotty ran through the densely-packed woodland as she had done countless times before, following the subject of her chase. As always, Dotty tried in vain to gain ground, to catch Sarah up. But it was no use. The girl simply melted away into the distance, leaving Dotty standing in a thicket with nothing but the whispering leaves for company.

And then suddenly Dotty felt a huge jolt, and without warning she was out of the woods and back in her bed. This recurring woodland vision she kept having, if it was a dream, was unlike any other she had ever had. Dotty could touch the forest – smell the pine and the damp earth so strongly that she could almost taste it. As if she really was there. In any case, wherever she had been, she was most definitely returned to her bedroom now, and it was as if she had never been in the forest at all.

Dotty lay there in her bed for a moment, confused, her senses taking their time to adjust to the change of scenery. Had she really been in a forest, or had her imagination simply taken the dark green damask of the drapes that enveloped her canopied bed as the inspiration for a vivid forest dream? She couldn't be sure, but her instincts told her there was something more to it.

It was early September and Dotty's room was stiflingly hot. When she had lived back in Cardiff, she didn't ever remember having experienced a summer like it. The air hung around her, thick and feverish, and sweat beaded her brow. If only for that reason, Dotty wished, just for a second, that she could be back in the forest of her visions. The climate there was quite cool and still: so very different from her hot, sticky room.

Perhaps if she pulled back the heavy curtains it would allow in a bit of a breeze. Dotty yanked irritably at the drapes. But opening them made no difference. Beyond the sanctuary of her four-poster lay simply more stale unmoving air. Of course, she could have opened the window. A little breeze might have helped. But Dotty didn't feel comfortable leaving the window open at night: not any more.

Dotty huffed impatiently, throwing herself back onto her pillows and then, rolling onto one side, punched a fist into them, trying to form a comfortable hole for her head. But she already knew it was no use. She was going to have to lay there until morning, awake, trying again to make sense of her recurring woodland vision. Just like she always did.

It always started the same. With Sarah: sweet gentle Sarah rousing her softly, as if from sleep, gesturing her to follow, urging her silently on, desperate to share a secret with Dotty, to show her – what? Something that Dotty never saw because she always lost the little girl in the clearing in the woods.

Dotty had tried to talk about it, thinking if she could just work through it with someone, that together they could make sense of it all, and somehow discover its meaning. But finding someone to talk with wasn't as easy as it sounded. Great-Uncle Winchester was his usual absent self, and as for Dotty's best friend, Sylv, she wasn't the most intuitive type. Perhaps Dotty was expecting a little much of Sylv in asking her to believe that there might be something otherworldly blurring the line between Dotty's dreams and reality in this hideous nightly theatre. But why did Sylv have to be so resistant to the idea?

The last time they had Skyped, Sylv had even got a bit ratty with her about it. Dotty remembered Sylv's looking decidedly exasperated as she stared out at Dotty from the screen of the iPad.

"Look, butt[1], it's simple. You're feeling guilty about Sarah. That's it. You want to save her from the hob. But you can't, and so in your dreams you keep re-living a situation in which she's just out of your reach. It's a classic 'dream anxiety manifestation.' Mam said so."

"You told your mam about this?" Dotty had been incredulous.

"Well, I was worried. You've been so weird about it. And I thought she might be able to help, being a doctor and all."

"Weird? And your mam isn't a doctor. She's a vet. There's a difference, you know. I'm not one of her depressed moggies, or dogs with body dysmorphia. I'm a human."

"All right, Dot, calm down, won't you? I was just trying to help."

---

[1] Colloquial Welsh for 'mate' or 'friend'.

Chapter 1

Dotty had sighed and, seeing that she was getting nowhere, had sensibly changed the subject.

Who knew, perhaps it was just a dream as Sylv said. But some nagging insistence in the back of Dotty's brain told her otherwise.

Pip was keeping his distance, too, which Dotty felt a bit hurt about. But then he had always been what her mam would have called a 'fair weather friend.' Between the lack of sleep and the lack of company, though, it really had been the worst summer she could recall, and Dotty would be glad to see the back of it.

If only she still had the Calendar House Key. Then she could use it to chimney hop and visit Sylv whenever she liked. How she hated that evil magpie, Mordecai, with his creepy mechanical eye, for stealing it from her. She hated him almost as much as she hated his master, the Vagabond King, who had instructed the awful bird to snatch it from her hand. Even now Dotty struggled to accept that the Key was now in the possession of those two, and she was terrified at the idea of what they might do with it.

In truth, she knew the crisis with the Key was the real reason why Great-Uncle Winchester and Pip had been so unavailable of late. They were busy working with the Sweep's Council to gather intelligence on the pair's whereabouts, and making contingency plans in the event of the Key's improper use. Assuming the Vagabond

King was going to use it, that was. After all, the Vagabond King's greatest desire was to sever all links between the world of sweeps and the world of men, so perhaps he had simply destroyed it. Dotty couldn't bear the thought of her mother's precious locket being smashed to pieces, though. The thought that it might be gone forever was just too horrible to bear.

So there Dotty was, stuck in Yorkshire, quite alone again, and with no way of getting out.

To add insult to injury, Sylv had been staying with her mam in Bristol all summer. Their flat was far too small and cramped to accommodate a guest, and Sylv hadn't been able to make the trip up to Yorkshire because her mam said she needed Sylv's help with the veterinary practice. Wanted, more like, Dotty thought. In any case, the consequence had been that Dotty had spent the whole holidays being bored and restless by day, and beset by strange and unfathomable visions at night. The whole thing was rotten.

Unable to get back to sleep, Dotty grudgingly pulled herself into a sitting position, swinging her legs over the side of the bed and feeling the relief of the cool wooden floor on her tired feet. It was too hot to bother with a dressing gown, so she left it and slouched straight down the back stairs.

Due to the early hour, Dotty had beaten Gobby into the kitchen and it was unusually empty. The lack of cook also meant breakfast wasn't yet on the go, so Dotty grabbed a crust of bread from the larder instead, and ambled off slowly down the corridor. Her head still full of her vision, she didn't notice Great-Uncle Winchester and Geoff the dog coming the other way down the passage, and when he boomed a morning greeting she almost jumped out of her skin with fright.

"Dear girl! How are you this fine morning?" Great-Uncle Winchester today was dressed as what appeared to be some sort of racing driver or pilot, with a leather helmet and goggles on his head. He was in his usual jovial mood, which irked Dotty all the more.

"What's fine about it?" she said, sulking.

Geoff bounded across to her, pushing his muzzle up under her hand for a stroke, but she pulled her arm away.

"The old boy only wants to say hello, you know." The old man gave her a look of fatherly concern. "I take it that dream of yours is still bothering you? Here, why don't you come into my study and we'll talk about it." He ushered Dotty into his room and gently closed the door behind them. "So tell me," he continued, settling himself down into his usual spot by the hearth.

Finally: someone who wanted to talk to her about her problem. Dotty jumped at the chance. "It's just the same thing every night," she answered. "And I know you all say it's just an anxiety dream – me working through my feelings about Sarah being taken by the hob and how I should have stopped it somehow."

"Darling girl, there was nothing you could do."

"Yes, I know – really I do. But it's not that. This dream, as you all call it: there's more to it. I really feel like I'm there in the woods with Sarah. And she's trying to tell me something, I'm certain."

"I believe that's what you want to think, my dear, but—"

"There's no 'but' about it!" Dotty was starting to get riled. "It's not a dream. It's real. I'm scared, Winnie. If only I could keep up with Sarah – find out what it is she wants."

Dotty's great-uncle gave her a hug. "Never you mind that. The important thing is that you are safe."

"Well, actually I'm more worried about Sarah than me. She needs me, somehow. I just don't know why."

Great-Uncle Winchester settled himself back into his chair. "Please be assured, my dear, if there was any hint of a cause for concern, I and the Council would be there like a shot. You must know that we would never allow you, or Sarah, to be put in harm's way – not for any reason."

Dotty exploded. "We? And just how, exactly, is the Council 'we'? Perhaps you could start by telling me that."

Chapter 1

"Dear girl?" Her great-uncle seemed taken aback.

"I've been here a year and I'm still none the wiser about this crazy old house and its weird and wonderful occupants than I was when I arrived. I mean, where do you—or is it we—fit in to it all? The hob called me a Guardian, but I don't know what that means. Are you and I some kind of gatekeepers to the world of sweeps, or what? I need to know."

Great-Uncle Winchester hesitated before answering. "Well, in a manner of speaking, yes, we are. Or I am, at least."

So there it was then: the truth at last. There was so much to know, to learn. But, before she could ask the thousand-more questions that came bursting into her head, Dotty's great-uncle spoke, his words careful and considered. "Darling girl, the situation is more complicated than you can know."

"I'm smart. I can learn."

"All in good time. And, my dear, I promise I will explain everything. But for now let us focus on the present situation. Perhaps give your troubling dreams an opportunity to subside, eh?"

"You can't keep fobbing me off like this!" she almost wailed in frustration.

Great-Uncle Winchester held her gaze. "Dotty. I will tell you everything. Just bear with me a little longer. Please."

Dotty rolled her eyes. "Fine." She got up to go. "If you don't have anything else to tell me about this guardian business, I'll be off.

"Hang on a minute, Dotty my dear. There was actually something I wanted to talk to you about as well."

"Oh?"

Great-Uncle Winchester looked troubled, pausing for a moment, as if trying to find the best way to frame what he was about to say "The thing is, darling girl, I think it's time you went to school."

Chapter 2

Ways and Means

On the outskirts of a small backwater town far from Yorkshire and the Calendar House, a travelling fair had set up shop. The night was fast approaching and the fairground was alive with colour and sound, busy with people visiting from all around.

Music played and machinery creaked and groaned as rides of all shapes and sizes circled round and round in endless journeys through the air. The wheels of a ghost train rattled along the tracks, its doors banging open and closed as it made its journey in and out of the haunted house ride that lay beyond its painted frontage. The air hung with the smell of engine oil and chip pans and the sugary promise of freshly-baked doughnuts.

In a far corner of the fairground, away from the bright lights and the bustle of the fairgoers, lay a small, square fortune teller's tent. Once brightly striped, its fabric was now old and faded, making it look as if it belonged to a travelling show that existed in a time long before this one. Above the tent's opening, which lay closed, hung a painted wooden sign, its letters cracked and peeling. To all intents and purposes, Madam Orla's tent had an air about it of an attraction that wished to be overlooked.

From within the tent there came the faint glow of a candle—although only one of the tent's occupants was in need of its light. Inside at a solitary table there sat an old crone, withered with age, her sightless eyes untroubled by the dimness of the light. Her companion's eyes were keen enough, although he too paid no mind to the lengthening shadows. The pair sat, deep in conversation.

"It is a long time since our paths have crossed," remarked the crone. "I was a young woman when last we met."

"Indeed you were, madam," replied the Vagabond King. "And you were quite beautiful then."

"I was, aye," the crone reminisced. "And quite the match for a fine man such as yourself." She sighed, clutching with gnarled fingers at the threadbare shawl that lay about her shoulders. "Alas. Age has not been kind to me," she said. "It has taken my looks, my loves, my eyes. I would that I could see how the years have changed your pretty face." She put her hand out to touch his cheek, but he drew away.

"Still, there is much to be grateful for," replied the King. "Your mind remains sharp, and you still have your living."

"Aye, such as it is." She gestured around her. "For that I should be grateful, at least." The woman poured some tea from an urn for the King, her fingers feeling for the rim of the cup that her eyes could not see. "So what is it you come here for?" she asked.

"I seek a favour, Madam. I have need of your otherworldly skills. Tell me, have you still a connection with the land of the Fae?"

The woman started. "The Fae? What business have you with them?"

"They possess something of mine," the King replied, "and I want it back. I am minded to pay them a visit."

"Making an enemy of the Fae—it is something I would ill advise."

"I do not seek your advice, old woman," replied the King. "My question is whether you can arrange passage for me."

Madam Orla leered, showing blackened gums, empty of teeth. "You want to enter the

Fae, eh? For you, my pretty one, I am sure I can find a way."

As quick as a flash, the old woman's hand shot across the table once more, grabbing a lock of the Vagabond King's hair and pulling it from its roots. The King winced slightly, but did not complain as she threw the hair into a small gold dish that sat on the table between them. Calmly, he sipped his tea as the woman applied her magic, taking from her dress pocket a box of matches with which she lit the contents of the dish. As the hair set alight the room was filled with the stench of burning hair, making the Vagabond King cough.

The woman seemed untroubled by the smell, however, and continued to talk as she worked. "A man of your knowledge and power will know that neither man nor beast can enter the world of the Fae directly when not invited. But there is a way you can follow one who has such an invitation, if you can find them."

The Vagabond King leaned back on his chair, watching lazily as the smoke rose up from the dish and made shadows in the haze: shadows that the old woman's blind eyes searched with interest, there seeming to find meaning.

"Aha," she said, smiling. "You are in luck. I see just such a person in the flames. 'Tis lucky she left a chink in the curtain as she passed through."

The King leaned forward. "Who is it? I cannot make it out."

Chapter 2

"Ha!" The crone chuckled to herself. "Come stand by me, pretty one. Take a look for yourself." She grabbed his hand as she spoke, but what she felt made her shrink back, afraid. "What manner of magic is this? Your flesh has not aged. It is as young and firm as we first met." She drew a cross upon her chest. "It seems to me you have already had much business with the Fae."

"It is no matter," replied the King. "Let me see." He peered into the smoke.

What he saw surprised him, and he rose so quickly from the table that he knocked over the bowl, scattering ash everywhere. "The Winchester girl!" he exclaimed. "I should have known. But how did she enter? I cannot let her take it."

"You know this girl?" asked the old fortune teller.

"Yes. She is, shall we say, the former owner of that which was taken from me."

The woman grinned. "I see – you have been dispossessed of something you first stole from her." She gave a cunning smile. "The item you seek must be something of great value to you. And such a thing should command a high price, don't you think?"

The Vagabond King sighed. "If you knew what it had already cost me."

"That is not my concern," replied the crone.

"So - can you do it?"

"Yes, I can do it. The magick you will need is a little tricky, but not impossible."

"Tell me." The King was more animated now, leaning forward eagerly in his chair.

The woman smiled once more. "And if I do? What would you offer me in return for this favour?" she asked. "Some of your youth, perhaps?"

"How about the gift of sight?" replied the Vagabond King, holding up in one hand his henchman's mechanical eye, idly swinging it by its thick leather strap.

Chapter 3

School

"School?" Dotty was shocked. She hadn't actually been to school since she'd moved up to Yorkshire over a year ago, and now it seemed that so much time had passed she had practically forgotten such a place existed. In Dotty's mind, school belonged to her old life back in Cardiff, not here.

Great-Uncle Winchester had broached the subject briefly once before, on Dotty's arrival at the Calendar House. But so soon after her parents' death, Dotty hadn't wanted to be thrust into yet another situation in which she knew no-one, and so she had resisted. She had been through so much already that her great-uncle had respected her wishes, notifying the local authority that she was to be home-schooled.

Not a lot of actual home-schooling had transpired since then. Great-Uncle Winchester was always so heavily preoccupied that Dotty easily managed to slip under the radar when it came to any formal plan of study. So Dotty's learning had come mostly in the form of Home Economics (baking) with Gobby, Science and Humanities with Kenny the gardener (potting out the seedlings and talking with him about the weather), and Information Technology (Skyping Sylv). She had to confess to have been sadly lacking in the English and Mathematics departments, however, unless you could include writing the odd letter, or counting out the change to give the butcher's boy.

Of course, as far as Great-Uncle Winchester and the House was concerned, Dotty had amassed a vast amount of information, both historical and metaphysical. But she didn't think that was exactly what the authorities would have had in mind.

"But why now?"

"My dear girl," began Great-Uncle Winchester. "It makes sense for you to start now that you're old enough to go to secondary school. I've kept you here for as long as I can, but don't you think it's time you went? Mixed with other young people? Get away from the house for a while?"

"I suppose, but…"

"There's a very good boarding school just a couple of hours down the road in Wakebury. It's…"

"Boarding school!" Dotty exclaimed. "Oh, it's like that is it? I have a few funny visions, become a problem to you, and suddenly you want to pack me off to school."

"Darling girl, no: nothing could be further from the truth. I very much want you to stay."

"I have a plan, you know. I'm going to catch up with Sarah next time. I'm sure I can if I try. You see, I know the route now: it's always the same. I can find out what she wants."

"Dotty, dear girl, it's nothing to do with your dream."

"It's not a dream – it's real." Dotty pouted. "Anyway, if it's not that, and if you really do want me around so much, why send me away?"

"I just think…well, you need to get out of the house for a while. It's for your own good."

"Then it must be something to do with my visions," Dotty persisted. "You think I'm in danger and you need me clear of the house. Or the Sweeps' Council is up to something and you don't want me to find out about it."

A small smile played around Great-Uncle Winchester's lips. "No, my dear, there is no secret plan afoot, and there is no immediate danger, I assure you."

"So then you do want to get rid of me. I was right. You think I'm going stir-crazy sat around in this big old house all day."

"There's more to it, dear girl."

Frustrated, Dotty threw her hands into the air. "Ugh! There always is." Dotty wished she could feel closer to her great-uncle: that he would let her in. It saddened her that, no matter how well they seemed to get on, she sensed him always holding something back, keeping her at arms' length, somehow.

"Dear girl – tell me you'll at least consider school? It's a very nice one. Your mother went there," he proffered.

"Don't you worry. I'll go. I know where I'm not wanted. After all, it can't be any worse than here." She was determined not to cry, but her bottom lip was beginning to tremble.

With a sigh the old man sat back in his chair. For a moment he hesitated, as if to say something more. But he didn't. Instead, with a great sadness in his eyes, he sat in impotent silence as his great-niece ran crying from the room.

Chapter 4

Uniform

"Unbelievable!" Sylv stared out from Dotty's iPad screen, wide-eyed. "So you're going to boarding school? When?"

"Term starts on Monday, apparently."

"But it's Thursday now!"

"Yeah. Nothing like a bit of short notice," Dotty replied tersely. "Gobby's taking me to get my uniform tomorrow."

"So what is the uniform like? I bet it's dead smart. Do you have to wear a straw hat and blazer?"

"Not in the September term," said Dotty, going a little red in the face.

"But aren't you looking forward to it, just a little bit?" Sylv asked. "I gotta tell you, I'm looking forward to starting big school. It'll be a big adventure. I mean, won't it be good to meet some new boys and girls, for you more than me? It'd be nice for you to have someone to talk to, other than your uncle and that crazy old cook, Gobby."

"You sound like Great-Uncle Winchester," Dotty replied. "And there aren't any boys. It's a girl's school." She blushed a little redder.

"No boys? Ha!" exclaimed Sylv. "It's one of them posh single-sex schools then? Like something out of one of them old movies your mam used to like – remember?"

"Of course I remember." Dotty looked sad. "She loved all that stuff. But no, it's very much in the here and now, Sylv. And I'm not looking forward to it. It's all right for you: there'll be a bunch of people you already know from St. Aidan's all going together. And you can come home at night. For me, well - I'll be the only one. And staying there, well it feels almost like moving house all over again. To tell you the truth, I'm scared."

"Aww, butt." Sylv touched the iPad screen. "Don't be. It'll be fun. Get you away from all the weirdness in the house. It'll be good for you."

"So everyone keeps on telling me," replied Dotty. But she wasn't convinced.

Chapter 4

Dotty sat and stared sulkily out of the window of the ancient Citroen 2CV as it creaked and rattled along the country roads towards Netherington and the school outfitters. The car belonged to Gobby, the Calendar House's cook-cum-housekeeper. Dotty had hoped to gain a sympathetic ear from the old woman during the journey, but as they had piled into the rickety old car, the suspension creaking and groaning under their combined weight, Gobby was, as ever, firmly behind her employer in his decision for Dotty to go to school.

"It'll—"

"Don't tell me," Dotty had interrupted grumpily. "Do me good. Yes, I know."

Gobby crunched through the gears and then sped off at a pace. They rattled along the lane, swerving from side to side as Gobby consistently took the corners too fast. Dotty grimaced.

"How far is it to Netherington, Mrs. Gobbins?"

"Not far. We'll be there in ten minutes."

"That's ten minutes too many," muttered Dotty under the sound of the engine.

"What's that, dear?"

"Nothing." Dotty muttered.

The car bounced into a stopping position in a cobbled bay immediately outside of a dreary-looking shop front displaying the uniforms of several different schools in its uninspiring window.

Uniform

Just as the car ground to a halt, as a prim-looking woman with her hair tied back in a bun opened the shop door with a *ting-a-ling* and gave Gobby her best smile. "Mrs. Gobbins, thank you so much for calling ahead. I am confident we will have everything you need here," she said. Then she eyed Dotty up and down as if pleasure was the last thing on her mind. "And this must be the, ahem—" she said, giving a small cough as if it pained her to say it, "—the young lady."

Dotty eyed the woman warily. The tape measure around her neck brought to Dotty's mind the image of a venomous snake draped about the shopkeeper's narrow shoulders.

Gobby beamed. "Thank you, Miss. Smart. Now you must let me introduce you. This is Mr. Winchester's great niece, Dotty."

Dotty smiled awkwardly. She looked as if she, or perhaps her tape measure, might bite.

"Do come in." Miss. Smart motioned them through the open door. Gobby stepped quickly inside and Dotty followed with much less enthusiasm.

The shop was filled from floor to ceiling with narrow shelves, stacked almost impossibly neatly, with an assortment of shirts and pullovers in every conceivable colour. Across the store there were hanging rails containing blazers and skirts, and there were wire bins filled with socks. A further rack that hung over a door contained a multitude of striped ties. And then Dotty noticed the hats, perched high atop the shelving, like a number of brightly-coloured straw birds. She cringed. Dotty absolutely hated hats. Hats and Dotty's hair just didn't go.

To be fair to Miss Smart, she was as efficient as her neat appearance suggested, and almost before Dotty could utter a complaint the woman had measured her from top to toe and, armed with a checklist, piled the counter high with a number of boxes containing neatly-folded skirts, shoes, knee socks, cardigans, various assorted items of sportswear, and even a woollen overcoat. Dotty noted with relief that she hadn't been forced to try any of the stuff on, at least. Perhaps this wasn't going to be such an ordeal after all.

Dotty was just about to heave a sigh of relief when the woman said, "I believe that is everything, Mrs. Gobbins, except for her hat."

Ugh - hats! "But I thought we only wore boaters in the summer?" Dotty exclaimed.

"Quite right, dear. In the winter you wear berets. Now let me just measure your head."

Berets? Dotty's stomach turned over. She knew for a fact that she would never be able to get a beret to stay on her head. Her wiry hair proved the most effective of headwear-repellents, any kind of hat just bouncing off it. This was the worst. Miss Smart took a blue corduroy beret down from a high shelf and brushed it into shape with a deft hand. "There. Shall we try it on for size?"

"It'll be fine." Dotty snatched it out of the surprised shopkeeper's hand.

"Well, I do say." Mrs. Gobbins gave the shopkeeper an effusive smile. "The girl must really like it."

Dotty muttered, "I'll be in the car," before heading for the exit as fast as her legs would carry her, the shop door *ding-a-linging* behind.

Sylv rolled around on her bed in a fit of laughing. Tears streamed down her face and she clutched her sides as she tried to catch her breath.

"You don't look so great either, you know." Dotty stood pitifully in front of the iPad which she had set up leaning against the bed post to give Sylv a full view of her uniform. It was Sunday evening, the night before both girls started their new schools. They had decided to put their uniforms on for the first time together: a decision Dotty was regretting.

"You gotta admit it is a bit funny." Sylv burst into another peal of laughter.

"Not seeing the funny side myself."

Dotty felt wretched. It was all right for Sylv. Dressed in grey from head to foot, with grey ribbed tights and black shoes, her uniform's only concession to colour was a red-and-gold striped tie. Sylv's uniform was boring, yes, but at least it wasn't interesting enough to be embarrassing.

Dotty's uniform on the other hand, with its gaudily-striped blazer, pleated kilt, and brown knee socks was almost too much for any self-respecting eleven-year-old to bear. And then there was the hat. No matter how hard she tried to pull it down onto her head, the corduroy beret remained uncompliant, perching on top of her hair in a most unflattering way, to all intents and purposes looking like Dotty was performing some kind of balancing act with it. There was no question in Dotty's mind. She was going to be the laughing stock of the school.

Sylv struggled to wipe the smile off her face, wiping a stray tear out of the corner of one eye. "On the bright side, Dot, at least you won't be the only one. All the other girls will be wearing one, too."

"But they don't have my hair, do they?"

"True. Perhaps try a couple of hair grips?" Unable to contain herself, Sylv started to giggle again.

Dotty pulled the offending article from its nesting place on the top of her hair and slumped down onto the floor, bringing the iPad with her so Sylv only had a view of her face.

"Spoilsport," pouted her friend cheerily.

"One good thing, at least," retorted Dotty. "I might meet some nicer friends."

Dotty's remark had the desired effect. Sylv now looking serious, asked, "We'll always be besties, though, won't we, Dot?"

"Sure, Sylv. We'll always be best friends."

Uniform

Chapter 5

First Day Nerves

Dotty had been worried that she was going to be a laughingstock when she arrived at the school gates in Gobby's comedy car, but luckily Great-Uncle Winchester had arranged for a school bus to come and collect her instead.

Dotty would have actually preferred her great-uncle to take her to school. Not that she was actually aware of him owning a car, now she came to think about it. But in the end it didn't matter because, true to form, he found an excuse not to take her. Sometimes Dotty wondered if Winnie cared about her at all.

Great-Uncle Winchester had asked Dotty to pop into his study and see him before she left.

But she had been so cross that she had made an excuse that the bus was ready to leave, and that she didn't have time. Of course, the bus would have waited for her, but she felt hurt and rejected, and hadn't felt like indulging him.

As she lived the farthest away from the school, Dotty was the first on the bus, and so she was able to get seated without fear of being teased. She settled down into a far corner and stuck her head in a book, sinking down into the seats slightly so as to draw least attention to herself. At least she didn't have to wear her hat during the journey.

It was about a two-hour trip to the school. After a short time, Dotty's book was unable to keep her attention. She must have been more tired than she had thought because she drifted off to sleep. When she awoke, the bus was full of girls of all ages, all wearing the same Wakebury School for Girls uniform as Dotty, and all staring at her, some with open mouths.

Dotty's first instinct was to put a hand to her head but, no, she had taken the horrid beret off when she had boarded the bus. Then, from amongst the gasps and titters of the assorted schoolgirls, somebody spoke. "Who's Sarah?" she asked.

"You were saying her name in your sleep," said another girl.

"Shouting it, more like," said a third.

Chapter 5

"Sarah, Sarah, come back!" an older girl mimicked Dotty's calls.

Dotty felt her face going hot. She bit her lip until it hurt. Please don't cry, she thought. Horrid girls. But before she could offer any retort, the driver called for everybody to get off the bus and the girls quickly turned away, pushing and shoving to get to their trunks, and Dotty was left sitting alone at the back, for the moment quite forgotten. Suddenly, facing the embarrassment of being dropped off at school in Gobby's silly car seemed as if it wouldn't have been such a bad alternative after all.

The rest of the day was a whirlwind of room maps and timetables, and new rules to learn, all of which took up too much of Dotty's time and energy for her to dwell on the unfortunate start to her school day. Lunchtime came and went without much of an incident, the girls filing in indiscriminately onto long trestle tables. The food wasn't bad, although the insipid sponge and watery custard was a poor substitute for Gobby's world-class treacle pudding.

It was after supper that things started to go badly wrong. The girls had been assigned to the various bedrooms, each having four beds. The girls were instructed to check the chart in the common room to see where they had been placed, their trunks having already been taken up for them. The girls crowded round the chart, Dotty hanging back a little to avoid the crush.

After a while Dotty became aware of some kind of kerfuffle involving two of the girls and the house mistress.

"But it's not fair, miss," one of them said.

"Why should we have to put up with her?" asked the second.

"She screams in her sleep."

"Yes, miss. I heard her on the bus, as plain as day," another girl chimed in.

"My father will hear about this," threatened the first girl again.

Dotty listened in horror as she realised the girls were talking about her. Less than twenty-four hours in the school and already she was a laughing-stock, a pariah. She took herself off to the toilets for a good cry.

The house mistress came to find her a little while later and was kind and made her a mug of hot chocolate, but Dotty felt as if the bottom had dropped out of her world. How was she ever going to settle in now, let alone make any friends? When she finally went up to bed two of the girls were either already asleep or pretending to be, and the third girl rolled over, turning her back to Dotty.

Dotty slipped under the covers and tried to snuggle down, but the bed felt small compared to the four poster she had at the Calendar House, and the mattress was so much harder than the domed feather mattress she had become used to.

Chapter 5

Oh what she would give for a comfortable, dreamless sleep.

"Good night," she whispered. But nobody replied.

First Day Nerves

Chapter 6

Through Smoke

It was a beautiful night. The sky was clear and bright, what remained of the summer still warming the earth, except in the dark places where the sun could not reach.

Raven's Fall was one such place. Long abandoned by men, its ruined battlements had not seen a summer for many generations. Jagged stonework lay overhung with brambles that seemed to cling to life in defiance of the sunshine that had forsaken them.

But hidden did not mean forgotten – not by the birds, at least. For the ruin was alive with them, and with untidy masses of fallen twigs, moss, lamb's wool stolen from the fields, and other assorted oddments spilling out of every crack and crevice. Such were their nests.

The birds cawed and bickered together in the darkness, all vying for the attention of their lord and master. Rooks fought and squabbled with crows and ravens with choughs, as they fawned and scraped over the great bird that held dominion over them.

Mordecai the Eyeless held court in the roofless space that would have once been the great hall of the castle. The great magpie towered over the other birds, his dirty, tattered plumage dwarfing the army of close to two hundred birds that surrounded him. In a corner of the room, a mouse strayed into the birds' midst, perhaps in search of food. As it sniffed the air, the huge bird became aware of the rodent's small, scampering movements and, with unnerving precision, Mordecai snapped it up by the tail, swallowing the mouse whole. Clearly the bird's blindness had not rendered him helpless. Far from it, his milk-white sightless eyes had ensured that his other senses were razor sharp—a fact of which his followers were all too aware.

Snack finished, Mordecai spoke. "Silence!" he commanded.

All the birds halted their in-fighting and turned to listen.

"The King will soon be here. Have the preparations been made?"

Chapter 6

"Yes, My Lord," piped up a small chough: a black bird, with a red beak and legs.

"And the fire: it is ready?" Mordecai asked.

"Yes, My Lord. We have made a fine fire of twigs collected from two of the largest nests, sacrificed for the purpose."

"Good. Now we wait. But give me quiet, so that I may hear him coming."

Not another bird spoke, and the room became unnervingly still.

Presently, a noise became apparent somewhere overhead, approaching from the east. The sound, which resembled a great number of wings flapping together, grew louder. "He is here," the magpie said.

Whatever scant light there had been in the castle glade was suddenly extinguished by an army of black wings circling in the air above. Slowly the swarming mass began to funnel downwards towards the ruin, descending like a winged tornado into the gloom. As each bird landed it pieced itself onto the next, merging into it to form a larger whole. The effect was to create a sort of grotesque living jigsaw of a man, all in black, his arms outstretched, holding aloft the folds of his great coat like a cloak. As the figure neared completion, he lowered his arms, the last of the birds flew into gaps and creases, to complete the last few pieces of the human puzzle. It was the Vagabond King.

In the presence of his master, the gargantuan bird's manner was noticeably less easy than it had been only moments before. Mordecai gave a low bow. "Welcome to Raven's Fall, master – as always, it is an honour to do your bidding."

The Vagabond King did not return his henchman's greeting. "Let's get on with it," he snarled. "You are ready to enter the Fae?"

"Yes, master." Mordecai bowed again as he spoke. "The fire is prepared, as am I."

"All right then. Just make sure you heed the words of the fortune teller. The portal will only stay open as long as the Winchester girl remains inside her vision. Do not let her see you – if she is startled, she may retreat from within it, and you will be cast out along with her."

The man bent down to the fire and, taking out a flint and steel, lit it with little effort. As the flames started to lick through the twigs the birds shrank away from it, one or two hopping from foot to foot in agitation at the heat of fire.

Only Mordecai did not draw back. The orange glow reflected in his white eyes and for that moment made them seem aflame, too.

The Vagabond King circled the fire, strange and powerful, muttering a string of words in an indecipherable tongue. As he spoke his strong, dark hands sprinkled something onto the burning wood. The fire spat and crackled, and the flames turned from red to blue. The smoke that hung above the fire grew thicker. Blue specks sparkled within it, making the smoke itself seem to glow from the inside out. Then through the smoke a vision appeared, hazy and half-formed: tall trees closely planted. The portal to the forest of the Fae was opened, just like Madam Orla had described. Now for Mordecai to enter.

The forest vision hung in the smoke, undulating as the heat rose up from the flames. But around its edges appeared something of which Madam Orla had not warned them. Strange shadows framed the portal, undulating in the haze, flickering like dancing sprites whirling around its borders. If the Vagabond King noticed the phenomenon, he chose to ignore it. Or perhaps it simply did not bother him. But the beady eyes of smaller birds saw the puzzling shadows, and began to whisper: unsettled, afraid.

"They are Wisps," they squawked, "spirits dancing at the edge of the nether world. This is not right. They will be freed." The birds continued to gossip and twitter quietly amongst themselves, but none spoke up to tell their master. As for Mordecai the Eyeless, who could not see the spectres playing at the vision's edge, he was too preoccupied with the task in hand to listen to their chattering.

The imposing figure of the Vagabond King circled the fire, completing his incantation.

"Go now, Mordecai," he said. "And remember: stay close to the girl, but do not let her see you."

Through Smoke

Mordecai croaked his acknowledgement. Then, launching himself into the air with a single flap of his great wings, he swooped down and, leaving Raven's Fall, he flew through the portal and into the Fae.

The other birds watched on as their master disappeared through into the shadowy woodland that rose above the flames, taking with him as he went both the smoke and the dancing spirits that circled the vision.

Chapter 7

Settling In

Dotty woke up to the feeling of someone tugging her gently by the arm, coaxing her out of sleep. As her eyes slowly came into focus she saw that it was Sarah who had roused her. Dotty stretched out her hands, palms down, and felt soft, wet grass beneath her. She was inside her vision again.

Sarah's mouth opened and closed, uttering soundless words. "Come on," she seemed to be saying, as she motioned Dotty to follow. Dotty got up, the damp ground feeling cold beneath the soles of her feet. Her thin cotton pyjamas clung to her legs. She shivered. Sarah pulled at her sleeve. "Come on," she mouthed. Dotty followed.

After so many of these visions, the path through the forest had become well-known to Dotty, and she felt more sure of the earth beneath her feet. It was becoming easier to keep up. She picked her way through the trees, able to navigate her path to the clearing by memory now. It was after that point that Dotty really needed to concentrate. She was determined not to lose Sarah this time. She had to find out what the little girl wanted: to help if she could, and, hopefully, to bring these terrible recurring visions to an end. It would be just as she had planned it: she would keep on running, blocking out everything around her and just focusing her eyes on the path ahead - on Sarah.

The planning paid off. On reaching the clearing Dotty managed to keep running, following Sarah as she sped through the woodland. Just as Dotty got the sense that there wasn't much further to go, Sarah came to a grinding halt, so that Dotty almost ran into her. The little girl turned, the moonlight silver on her face, ghostly. Her long hair brushed against Dotty's cheek, tickling Dotty's face. "Shhh," she mouthed, placing long, slender fingers on Dotty's lips.

Dotty shuddered at Sarah's touch, so cold and real. These visions: she knew they were so much more than just dreams. Sarah really was reaching out to her – communing with her from the Fae.

Chapter 7

Turning, Sarah pointed to something up ahead. There was some kind of light glowing in amongst the trees. Dotty strained hard, trying to get a clearer look. She made to move closer, but Sarah put a hand up to stop her. She shook her head at Dotty, clearly fearful of what lay beyond.

Dotty squinted to get a better view. The light seemed to be coming from one tree in particular: an unnatural blue light that Dotty had seen before. It was the light that had come from the hob when it had come to take Joe's soul. But of course the hob had not taken him. It had taken Sarah instead.

Dotty inched forward, just half a step. Sarah looked alarmed, shaking her head and motioning that they should stay hidden. But Dotty smiled at her gently, reassuring her. "It's okay – I just want to see a little better."

The tree with the strange blue light seemed to be hung with a collection of ornaments of sorts: trinkets and other random items - a snuff box, some spectacles, a pocket watch. It was indeed an odd thing. The branches of the tree itself appeared dead: a skeleton or shell of something that once lived. Or perhaps it had never had life of its own. But the items that adorned it each exuded a glow of life: their collective presence upon its branches giving the tree a sense of life more abundant than reigned anywhere else in the forest. It was as if, together, these things gave the tree its own life-force or power.

Dotty examined the assorted oddments that decorated the tree. It was then that she saw it: her mam's locket. But surely not: no, it couldn't be. Was that really the Calendar House Key hanging from a tree in the middle of the forest? It just didn't make sense. In a dream, she could have understood its presence: dreams never made sense. But if, as Dotty suspected, this really was the forest of the Fae that she was seeing first hand, how on earth did the locket get there? The last she knew it was in the possession of the Vagabond King.

Lost in the moment of her discovery, Dotty forgot Sarah's warning to remain hidden and stood up. There was a tiny sound behind her: the tell-tale crack of a twig breaking under foot, alerting Dotty to the presence of someone with them in the forest – something or someone that had followed her into the woods in her pursuit of Sarah. She felt a rush of movement behind her. But even as she turned around a noise from beyond the Fae pulled her out of her vision.

It was someone crying. At first Dotty was afraid that her own cries had been the cause of her waking. She scanned the dormitory, panicked, looking for the angry faces of her roommates, roused from their beds by another of Dotty's outbursts. But if she had been making a noise, it had not disturbed them, as they were all still asleep. All except one. In the far corner a short red-headed girl, the one whose name was Lucy, or Laura, Dotty thought, was weeping. She was trying to hide it but her shoulders trembled and Dotty could see that she was upset, even in the dark.

"Are you okay?" Dotty ventured. The girl sobbed quietly to herself. Tentatively, Dotty got out of bed and tiptoed across the room. "What's wrong?" she asked, sitting down beside the crying girl. "Is there anything I can do to help?"

"No," replied a small voice. "Thank you. I'm just homesick, that's all. I miss my mum and dad. And Archie – my dog."

"I miss my parents, too," said Dotty, speaking the truth. She gave the girl's hand a small squeeze. "It'll be okay. We're all in this together," she said, slipping off the bed. "Try to get some sleep now. Things'll look better in the morning, I'm sure."

"I'm Lara," said the girl.

"Dotty."

Exhausted from her night time adventures, Dotty climbed back into her own bed and drifted into a dreamless sleep.

Dotty awoke the next morning in a considerably better frame of mind than she had been the day before. It was amazing how having a friend could make you see things so much more positively. She looked at the little alarm clock she had placed at her bedside the night before. It was 7.45 a.m. already. She must have overslept. This was the first time Dotty had slept past 6 in a long time. Dotty glanced at the other beds and was surprised to see that two of the girls – the ones who had complained about sharing a dorm with her - were still in them. She felt slightly better to think that they must have overslept as well. But then she supposed their first day at school had been a tiring one, too. Dotty considered waking them but, keen not to annoy them more than she already had done, decided against it.

The bed where Lara slept was empty, so at least someone was up. Dotty heard the shower going in the girls' shared bathroom and concluded that it must be her. After a short while, Lara emerged, towelling wet hair. She smiled sheepishly. Dotty noticed the abundance of freckles that covered almost every inch of the girl's face.

"Morning," said Dotty, deciding for that moment not to elaborate on the night before. She gestured towards their sleeping roommates. "I was wondering if we should wake them? Only…"

"You don't want to," replied Lara. "I can understand why. Fliss and Tory weren't very nice to you yesterday, were they?"

"Oh, is that their names?" Dotty smiled awkwardly. "Well, I guess they don't know me yet. And I must have looked a bit of a fool on the bus."

Chapter 7

Lara giggled. "Just a bit. Don't worry, I'll do it - Fliss first, I think," she gave the girl nearest to her a shake. Fliss didn't stir. Lara gave Dotty a quizzical look, and then shook the girl again. "Fliss, are you awake?" Still no movement. "Heavy sleeper, I guess." She added, "I wasn't sure whether she was awake or not because her eyes are open."

Dotty leaned over to have a look, and pulled a face. "Yew -gross!"

Lara grabbed a corner of the quilt that covered the sleeping girl. "Okay then. How about something a little more extreme?" In one swipe, she pulled the covers clean off the bed, leaving the girl lying prone on the thinly-covered mattress.

Zero reaction.

Now Dotty was beginning to worry. She grabbed Fliss's motionless body and together she and Lara proceeded to shake Fliss vigorously. But it seemed nothing would rouse her.

"Let's try Tory." Dotty ran to the other bed, and gave its occupant a rough shake, but Tory did not wake either.

Dotty stared at the girl, a knot forming in the pit of her stomach. "Lara, you need to see this. Tory's got her eyes open, too."

This was bad. Dotty couldn't quite put her finger on it yet, but a little voice in the back of her head told her there was something otherworldly about this. Worse than that — she couldn't fight the growing suspicion that somehow the unnatural sleep of the two girls was connected to her waking dreams, or visions, or

whatever on earth they were. After all, hadn't she had a vision last night?

Dotty glanced at Lara, who was beginning to look panicked. "Dotty, you don't suppose they're...?"

"No. They're breathing." Dotty reassured her. "They just seem to be asleep, only - with their eyes open."

Lara heaved an audible sigh of relief.

"I still think we'd better call Matron, though."

Chapter 8

Into the Fae

The smoke billowed around Mordecai the Eyeless as he flew noiselessly through the void that separated the land of the Fae and the world of men. As he beat forward on strong wings the swirling mist began to clear, lifting with it the fog from his sightless eyes, so that little by little the bird began to see.

Mordecai hesitated for a moment, perhaps unsure whether this was the sight that returned to him in his dreams at night, or whether it was the act of entering the Fae that had itself performed some sort of miracle. No matter – the blind and sorry version of himself that lived in the world of men was gone. Here in the forest, not only was his sight returned to him, but his black and white feathers were as sleek and as bright as they had been in the first flush of his youth, and his eyes were as sharp and as piercing as the cut of his beak.

Renewed in vigour he surged ahead, looking for a sign of movement in the trees. At first he saw nothing, but then, just up ahead, he saw a flash of something white streaking through the trees. It was a girl, running barefoot through the forest, her thin cotton pyjamas snagging and tearing on thorns and bushes as she stumbled through the undergrowth. This is what he sought – the girl from the Calendar House – the one who would lead him to the token that his master craved so badly.

Mordecai forged on, trying to gain on his target. He could smell her now, and hear her breathless calls, and beneath that her heartbeat.

Suddenly the girl stopped dead, crouching low between the trees. Mordecai touched down on the forest floor; a mistake, as a dry twig cracked under his foot, threatening to give away his position. But if his quarry heard it, she did not turn around. He homed in, almost upon her. She was looking at something that lay beyond. It was some sort of tree – bewitched with strange magic that made it glow with a queer blue light. Hanging from each of its branches were trinkets, some shiny and attractive to him, some less so. The bird scanned through the assortment of oddities, searching for a small gold locket: the one that his master had lost. Could the Calendar House Key really be there? Could it be this simple?

All at once the girl stood up, exclaiming her surprise to see her mother's locket sitting in the boughs. Mordecai hesitated, bracing himself in case the girl broke from her vision. But for the moment she did not. He must act now or risk losing his prize. The great bird swept forward, his sights beyond the girl now, focused only on the Key.

But just as he took to the air, without warning the light in his eyes was snuffed out, and world became black. What had just happened? Had the girl's vision been broken? Interrupted somehow? Disoriented, he felt himself tumbling, falling through the darkness until he found himself being roughly ejected through the portal and back into the world of men. Unprepared for the rough manner of his exit from the Fae, the bird landed heavily onto the glowing embers of the fire, which now burned hot again. He squawked in shock and pain as he hopped from foot to foot in the burning ash, unsure for a moment which was right or left, up or down. But then a red-footed chough and a raven came to his rescue, pulling him away from the fire.

"Master, do you have it? Do you have the locket?" they asked him.

"A moment, please. Leave me be," he commanded, as he gathered himself.

"He does not have it. He returns without it," a little bird piped up.

"The King will be in a fury." The birds began to twitter between themselves, the air filling with an anxious frenzy. "We will know his anger."

"I was cast out," the magpie replied, tending to his poor burned feet. "As the crone warned us. The girl awoke from her vision. It is the magick's fault, not mine."

"But you saw the locket? It is there?" a voice came from the dark, interrupting them. The Vagabond King stepped out of the shadows.

"Y..y..yes, Master," Mordecai said, cowering beneath him. "I saw the Key, but something woke her. The spell was broken."

"Then it looks like you are going to have to go back."

The birds started chattering again. "It is bad magick," one said.

"There are spirits," said another.

"Yes, there are wisps," said a third.

"What mean you?" Mordecai asked.

"The spirits of the fire: they followed you. You should not return to the Fae."

"Too dangerous," they all started squawking.

Mordecai ignored them, replying to his master. "Of course I will return. I will not fail you a second time."

"Your word is your bond," said the King in reply. And with that he rose up into the night sky, his body consumed in a thunder of beating wings,

Chapter 8

leaving his broken, tattered henchman to tend to his blackened claws.

Into the Fae

Chapter 9

Witch!

Upon the discovery of the sleeping girls, a predictable amount of drama ensued, with doctors being called and then ambulances, the Health Authority and finally parents being informed. The atmosphere in the school was tense: with girls and staff both equally unnerved by the morning's discoveries. The teachers seemed distracted as they gave their lessons, and it was clear that their pupils were struggling to concentrate, too.

At first there was rumour of an illness: some unnamed virus that had taken over the school. The girls talked stiffly and politely to one another, trying not to get too close, and the staff room was a hotbed of discussion over whether the Health Authority would call for the school to be quarantined or closed.

In the end, it seemed that both measures were to apply. The Authority was quick to confirm that they could find no evidence of infection, but followed this with an announcement that the premises would have to be swept for signs of a stray toxin that might have found its way into the school and caused the girls' comatose condition. Pupils and staff alike were confined to their common rooms whilst the grounds were scoured. If a toxin was found, the school would be closed.

The search only took an afternoon but, to Dotty, it seemed like it would never end. With nothing better to do, the waiting girls sat around discussing the mystery illness, and conjecture quickly gave way to idle gossip. This in itself wouldn't have mattered, except that, to Dotty's surprise and annoyance, she found herself once more becoming the topic of conversation in her common room.

"Of course, they won't find anything," one girl started.

"Yeah, everyone knows it's not an illness," said another, "it's a curse. Made by a witch."

"Yeah, and we all know who that is."

"Dotty." The girls carried on with their chatter, as if Dotty wasn't even there.

Lara spoke up, "Don't be daft. What on earth would make you think that?"

The girl who had started the conversation spoke up. "Isn't it obvious? She has been communing with the spirits in her sleep. We saw her as clear as day. Babbling on the bus to her familiar, Sarah."

"This is ridiculous!" Dotty huffed, crossing her arms defensively. "You're all being stupid." But even as she spoke, Dotty couldn't help but feel that the two 'sleep' related incidents were more than a coincidence. Perhaps the girls were right – this was all Dotty's fault.

Just like they had on the bus, the other girls pointed and stared at her. Only this time, no one laughed. Even Lara seemed not to be able to find the words to defuse the situation. If Dotty could have fled the room, she would have. But whilst the search of the school continued, they weren't allowed to leave. So Dotty just sat in the corner, wishing fervently that the ground would swallow her up.

When finally the Authority confirmed that they could find nothing of concern in the grounds, and pronounced the incidents were isolated, this should have been a cause for celebration. But as everyone piled down to the refectory for supper the mood was distinctly muted.

The loose tongues of the girls meant that the conversation that had taken place in Dotty's common room spread through the dining hall like wildfire. As a result, with the exception of Lara, no one would sit with Dotty at the dinner table. Worst of all, though, was that Dotty was beginning to believe that they were right, and that she really had bought a curse upon the school.

Chapter 10

Homework

Supper was finished, and Lara disappeared to phone her parents, leaving Dotty to walk alone back up to the dorm. Dotty didn't have much of a sense of direction at the best of times and, in consequence, her route was somewhat circuitous. She found herself walking through the wide panelled hallway that cut through the middle of the main school building, a space which she recognised at least, and from which she could gather her bearings. The corridor was filled on either side with large glass cases, framed in dark wood, containing silver and gold cups, silk rosettes, and all manner of other school memorabilia. Dotty stopped to look in one or two of them, figuring there was no need to rush back to her room since she was hardly expecting a warm welcome when she got there.

In the display case she saw an old photograph of the under-16s' netball team holding a large shiny cup. There was a newspaper clipping pasted onto a card next to it. It showed a girl holding the cup, together with a woman in an academic cape, presumably the then-headmistress, and two men – one older, one younger. The girl's netball bib read "W A". Wing attack – the same position Dotty had played back in Cardiff. Gosh, that seemed like a long time ago. The headline read as follows.

"Wakebury Wins Inter-County Cup. Pupil scores record number of goals."

Dotty read on.

> *"Fifteen-year-old Gwendoline Winchester today saved the day, scoring a record number of sixteen goals for her team at Wakebury Girls' and bringing them into first position to win the coveted Northern Inter County Cup."*

Gwendoline Winchester! That was Dotty's mother, although everyone had called her Gwennie. Dotty looked more closely at the clipping. She hadn't seen many photographs of her mother as a young girl. The quality wasn't very good, and it was in black and white, but she could still make out Mam's young face smiling out from the picture. So who were the two men with her? Presumably her mam's father and, oh yes, Great-Uncle Winchester. She smiled to see a familiar face. He hadn't changed a bit in all these years.

But, hang on a minute, that couldn't be right. If Great-Uncle Winchester was her mother's uncle, then he would have been a similar age to his brother, Gwennie's father, give or take a year or two. The man in the photo was the same age as her great-uncle was now. So maybe he was her mother's grandfather, Dotty's great-grandfather. Wow, some family resemblance.

Dotty made it back to the dorm without further hitch but she remained intrigued by the photograph of her mother and her family. It occurred to her that she hadn't ever asked her great-uncle if she could see any photographs of the Winchester family. She supposed that until now it had all been a little too raw; that to see photographs of her mother as a child might remind Dotty too keenly of her recent loss.

But now Dotty was intrigued to see more of the family she had never known, and to find out what she could about them, particularly in light of Great-Uncle Winchester's shock revelation about him (and possibly her) being some sort of guardian to the sweep world. She wondered if guardianship was something that was passed down through the generations. If that was the case, wouldn't her mother would have been one, too?

Dotty's questions about the guardianship issue might have had to wait until she got home, but she was in considerably more luck in respect of her mother's picture in the hallway. As luck would have it, in the very next lesson the teacher announced that they would be doing a genealogy project for the duration of the winter term.

"We're going to be practising our detective skills finding out about our own families' histories," explained the ancient tweed-suited history teacher, Mrs. Price. "Have you ever wondered if you might be related to kings or queens, or perhaps even a Viking? I have. Maybe you've heard a story about a soldier in your family who fought in a war, or you have the same last name as somebody famous and you'd like to find out if you're related."

Or maybe your family members are guardians to a magical world of sweeps that live inside your house, thought Dotty, allowing herself a small smile.

"Ah yes, Dotty," Mrs Price turned to her. "Why don't we start with you. What can you tell me about your family's history?"

"Well, I don't know much, miss. My parents died and I live with my uncle." A murmur rippled across the classroom. Dotty did her best to ignore it.

"But there is a photograph – here in the hall," Dotty continued. "I saw it yesterday. Of my mother and my grandfather and great-grandfather," she said.

"Of course," the teacher chimed in. "You're Gwendoline Winchester's daughter. I remember her well. A fine netball player, as I remember. Does it run in the family, I wonder?" She smiled convivially at Dotty.

Dotty looked hard at the ground. She loved netball, but she didn't want to say so in front of the class. She didn't want to do anything that might draw any more attention to herself, frankly.

Seemingly unaware of Dotty's discomfort, the teacher continued. "But if I recall, that isn't your great-grandfather in the picture. It was Gwendoline's uncle. I remember him quite distinctly because he was such a character, what we old folk might call an eccentric. You never knew what he was going to be dressed in when he turned up at the school—tennis flannels one day and a fisherman's hat the next."

Dotty stared at the teacher, agog.

"Yes," the teacher said, reminiscing. "They simply referred to him as Winchester: Great-Uncle Winchester."

Well, that cinched it. Not only did everyone think Dotty was a witch, but now it appeared that she had a great-uncle who was about million years old. What was she? Part of the Addams family or something? Dotty didn't know what to say. She went beetroot-red. She sensed everyone was staring at her again.

"So, girls," Mrs. Price finished up. "Speak to your parents or guardians and ask if they can help you dig out some photographs of the family." She smiled pointedly at Dotty as she said this. "Then you can bring them to school to put on your family tree board. Dotty, you might find some more of your mother," she finished kindly.

Dotty thought she was going to find a lot more than that.

Chapter 11

A Visitor

The dorm was distinctly quiet that night, with two of the four beds being empty. Although Dotty wasn't used to having a lot of company, she found it eerily quiet.

Lara was downstairs speaking to her parents again, so Dotty had the room to herself. It was still early, so she donned her dressing gown and settled herself down on top of the covers to read a book. Suddenly, there was a rustle in the fireplace, and then a small shower of soot fell down the chimney and landed in the grate, creating a cloud of black dust over the fireside rug. Dotty squeaked in surprise. She already knew what it was, but somehow she hadn't expected to see him in school.

A second later, Pip landed neatly on the hearth. He gave his standard greeting. "Evening, miss."

"Pip!" Dotty started, "are you mad? What are you doing here? Everyone around here thinks I'm crazy enough as it is! It's lucky there's nobody about." She looked around the room nervously, as if expecting a stray student suddenly to appear.

Pip looked puzzled. "Why do people think you're crazy?" He waved the question away. "Never mind. I'm here to give you a jolly good telling off."

Dotty looked at him crossly. "And I suppose Great-Uncle Winchester sent you?"

"No, actually, I came on my own. But it's him that I'm here about."

Dotty huffed.

"Why didn't you come and say goodbye? He wanted to see you. He's really upset, you know."

"He's upset?" Dotty folded her arms defensively. "He's not the one who's been packed off to boarding school at the first sign of an odd funny dream."

Pip gave her a look. "I thought they was visions, not dreams? And I know you're angry with him and you think he's abandoned you, but I'm here to tell you that you're wrong. What he's doing is only to protect you. You are more precious to him, to all of us, than you could possibly know. Besides, I thought you'd told him you were happy to go to school."

Dotty wasn't going to surrender her position without a fight. "Well, I wasn't. And as for feeling precious – I don't. I just feel left in the dark. All anyone ever tells me is half-truths. I know I'm a guardian, or that Great-Uncle Winchester is, at least. But not because he told me; I was told *that* by a hob, some kind of powerful faerie that I never knew existed before I came to live at that crazy old house. And if he is a guardian: so what? I don't know what it means. I asked, but as usual my great-uncle, who you think so highly of, wouldn't tell me."

Pip interjected. "He's a good man, Mr. Winchester. You just have to learn to trust him a bit more, is all."

Dotty pouted. "I seem to be expected to take a lot on good faith around here, but I'm not being given anything back. And then there's the photograph. I mean, just how old *is* Great-Uncle Winchester, anyway?"

"You don't give up, do you?" Pip sighed. "Okay, I take your point and perhaps he does need to tell you more. But he's been on his own a long time, you know. He's adjusting, too. And no matter what, he's still family. He loves you and he needs to know you're okay. So just speak to him, all right?"

Dotty swallowed back a sob. In truth, she was feeling terrible about not saying goodbye. She slumped down on the bed. "The thing is, Pip, I'm really not okay. Something very bad is going on here. My roommates wouldn't wake up and the school's been up in arms and I just know it's connected to my visions somehow and, well - what if they're right? What if the whole thing is all my fault?"

"Not to offend you, miss, but I just can't see the logic in that. Why should your visions be linked to what has happened to these girls?

Dotty sighed. "Just a feeling, I guess."

"Look," Pip said, his tone softening. "I get it. You've been through a lot over the last few months. But you're speaking to the wrong person. You should write to Mr. Winchester about it. Tell him, if you really do think there's a connection. He can run it by the Council – get you some reassurance, at least."

Dotty scowled at him. "Fat lot of use you are." Pip was right, though. She had been a bit hard on the old man. And she would certainly feel a lot better having spoken to someone about her worries. It wasn't as if she could run her suspicions past anyone here – they already thought she was bonkers. Anyway, if she and her visions were responsible for the mystery illness, she really needed to warn someone before it happened again.

"Okay, you can consider your job done. I'll write to Great-Uncle Winchester in the morning. Promise."

"I'm glad, miss. It'll mean a lot to him." Pip doffed his cap politely and was off back up the chimney again.

With Pip gone, Dotty settled herself down to sleep. She was quickly immersed into the nightly repeat of her strange woodland vision. But this time it was different than before. It wasn't what happened in the vision – that stayed the same, with Sarah leading her silently to the glowing blue tree hung with strange artifacts, and the Calendar House Key. But the dream *felt* different.

It could have been Dotty's concern about how her visions might be affecting those around her that gave her surroundings a new sense of foreboding. Or it could have been the fact that she now recognised that she was being followed – pursued by something that flitted through the trees behind her. But it seemed to her that the woods were somehow alive where before they had not been; and that a whole host of creatures resided hidden under the darkened canopies: dancing in the shadow of the leaves, but always just out of her line of vision.

Whatever it was, it made Dotty feel less safe in the woods than she had done before. It was unnerving and she didn't like it one bit.

Dotty awoke the next morning feeling better that she was going to break her silence with Great-Uncle Winchester. Although she had been annoyed with Pip for sticking his nose in the night before, she was glad that he had. It would be good to talk to someone about all the strange goings-on. She would write straight after breakfast.

Quickly she donned her uniform and dragged a brush through her unruly hair before heading down to the refectory. But when she got there, all thoughts of letter writing were instantly forgotten as she was met by a sea of wild-eyed angry faces. Dotty hesitated, debating what to do. She took a few paces towards the stack of breakfast trays, but two older girls barred her way, arms crossed aggressively in front of them.

"Witch!" one of the girls shouted.

Dotty took a step back, shocked.

"What have you done this time?" another accused.

Dotty searched the sea of faces for help, a teacher perhaps. But she couldn't immediately see anyone. At that moment a red head bobbed through the hostile mob, and with relief, Dotty saw that it was Lara.

"What's going on?" Dotty asked.

Lara grabbed her by the hand and marched her out of the room, pushing past a couple of taller girls, talking quickly as they went. "Come with me. You really don't want to be in there right now."

"You've got some guts," said Dotty, impressed. "What's wrong with them all? Have they all gone mad?" she asked as she allowed Lara to pull her along by the sleeve.

"No. They're scared," Lara replied. "Another two girls have taken ill."

Dotty felt her knees buckle under her, but Lara grabbed her before she fell.

"Hey, Dotty. You alright?"

"Yeah, sure. I'm fine." But, in truth, Dotty didn't feel fine at all.

There was no question that the school should stay open after that. The girls' parents were notified that, until the source of the epidemic could be discovered and the matter resolved, the school would be closed immediately.

From then on, a continuous stream of parents seemed to be arriving by the truck load to remove their precious offspring. As the mass exodus unfolded, the school went into full alert. Experts were sent in from the Health Authority to check everything: the food, the water supply - even Mrs. Boston's chemistry lab came under scrutiny. All the school could do was to wait impatiently for a decision from the experts as to the source of the outbreak.

Great-Uncle Winchester offered to send a car for Dotty, but she said there was no need. She would have jumped at the offer of a lift if he was collecting her himself, but as he wasn't she stubbornly figured she'd rather make her own way home.

A Visitor

In truth Dotty couldn't wait to get back to the Calendar House. It had been a rotten start to her school life in Yorkshire. Of course, unlike the other girls, it wasn't that she was scared that she would become a victim of the strange illness. On the contrary, much as she hated to side with her classmates, she couldn't help but feel that the sleeping sickness that was taking over the school and her visions were somehow connected. It seemed obvious to her that something more magical than a common cold was at work here. Whatever was going on, Dotty felt at least partly responsible, and that was killing her.

Still, things could have been worse at school – at least she had found an ally in Lara. The two were quickly becoming firm friends, which was just as well because Dotty thought that, if it wasn't for Lara, her experience of Wakebury Girls would have been quite simply unbearable.

Chapter 12

Back Home

The Health Authority had requested that nothing be removed from the school, including the pupils' own trunks, so the girls were sent home with only the clothes on their backs. From Dotty's perspective, this made things a whole lot easier as, with no heavy bags to lug around, it meant she could more easily take the train. The train was slightly quicker than the bus, but more importantly it would also spare Dotty from spending a full two hours in closed quarters with a bunch of glowering schoolgirls. It was a win-win situation.

Even better than this, Dotty was very pleased to find that she would be sharing part of her journey with Lara, who was going to get off only a couple of stops before her.

"My mum and dad were desperate to collect me," Lara had admitted. "But I told them I didn't want you travelling on your own." Thank goodness for Lara.

After boarding the train together, the rickety old train took the girls across the countryside and through endless little stations, quite different to the mainline service that had first brought Dotty to Yorkshire. It was a pleasant journey home, with Dotty mostly listening to Lara prattle on contentedly about seeing her parents and Archie the dog. Consequently time went quickly and Dotty was disappointed when her friend had to get off the train. Both Lara's mum and dad and the dog, which was a small brown terrier of sorts, were at the train station waiting for her. Dotty watched a little sadly out of the window as Lara's parents simultaneously scooped their daughter up into their arms, her mother crying with relief.

Lara turned to wave and Dotty returned the goodbye, all at once feeling lost and alone. She expected Gobby would meet her at the small station in Netherbridge. Dotty recalled when she had first arrived at the Calendar House. Gobby had collected her from the station then, too. The cook had stood on the platform waving comically at her, a rolling pin in her pocket and covered with flour. She was a funny old bird. Still, it would have meant the world to Dotty if Great-

Chapter 12

Uncle Winchester had come himself, and it saddened her that he chose not to.

Nobody was more surprised than Dotty, then, when she clambered off the train to find someone altogether different lurking in the shadows by the station exit.

"Pip?" Dotty always found it disconcerting to see Pip any distance away from a chimney or, indeed, outside the Calendar House. She looked around for evidence of his broom.

Pip beamed at her. "Miss," he said, doffing his cap.

"No Gobby?" asked Dotty.

"Well, actually, that's what I'm here about."

Dotty was alarmed. "Oh my goodness, why? Is she all right? Nothing's happened to her, has it?"

Pip grinned. "Not exactly, but she has gone a bit bonkers. Refused to leave the kitchen. We're putting it down to the excitement of you being home. She's really missed you, you know."

"But it's only been three weeks!"

"Well, that's Mrs. Gobbins for you."

"Pip, how are we going to get there? Home, I mean? You haven't forgotten that I can't chimney hop any more, have you?"

"Of course not, miss," Pip replied. "I thought we'd walk. It's not that far as the crow flies. Just a few miles across a couple of fields then there's an underground passage we can use as a shortcut for the last bit."

Miles? Dotty had a better idea. "Forget that. I'm hailing a cab."

There was a taxi rank just outside the station exit and Dotty quickly found a waiting car, which she proceeded to climb into the back of. "Come on, Pip. Let's go."

Pip looked nervous. "But how are we going to pay for it?"

"Oh don't worry about that. I'm sure Great-Uncle Winchester won't mind stumping up the cash when we get there."

"I'm really not sure, miss." Pip hesitated.

Dotty looked at him squarely. "You're afraid!" she accused. "Pip, haven't you been in a car before?"

"Newfangled contraptions," he grumbled. "Downright dangerous, if you ask me."

"Says the boy who travels up and down chimneys at the speed of light for a living. Really?" Dotty laughed at him. "Don't' be daft. Get in," she insisted.

The ten-minute ride wasn't entirely without incident, as a very green-looking Pip had to stop at the side of the road twice to be sick. Dotty found this hysterically funny, although the taxi driver clearly didn't share the joke, as he kept on making threats about cleaning charges and his upholstery.

By the time they got to the house, Pip had clearly lost his sense of humour, as well as his breakfast and possibly his lunch. He skulked off

Chapter 12

without much of a goodbye, other than to warn

Dotty to stay away from the kitchen – a warning which of course Dotty ignored.

But as soon as she arrived at the kitchen she realised exactly what all the fuss had been about. Gobby was clearly in the grip of a monumental baking frenzy. The place looked like a bomb had hit it. This was much more than the usually ample dusting of flour that covered the surfaces. It appeared that Gobby had used every conceivable dish and utensil in the cavernous kitchen in pursuit of her latest endeavour. Whatever was she doing?

A plume of steam erupted out of one of the cooking pots that sat on the stove, Gobby emerging soon after it from behind one of the huge oven doors. She was heavily laden with a baking tray full of cookies of some description. On seeing Dotty the cook promptly dropped the tray with a shriek, sending hot biscuits scattering all across the stone floor. "You're here," she said in surprise.

"Yes. I thought you were expecting me."

"Of course, dear. It's just that I thought you would be a little longer. I must have lost track of time. Dear me." She looked at the devastation on the worktops. "I don't think I'm quite ready."

"Ready for what?"

"Why, for your homecoming, of course." Gobby left the biscuity-mess that lay strewn around her and in a flash was enveloping Dotty in one of her trademark floury hugs. Dotty couldn't help but smile. As usual, Gobby smelled amazing. Dotty felt as if she could lose herself forever in one of those hugs. But as quick as the cook was to embrace Dotty, she was off again, tending to pots, pans, and kettles.

"Pity about those," said Gobby, eyeing the mess on the floor. "Aberffraw biscuits. Said to be the oldest biscuits in Britain: an old Welsh recipe. But then you'd know that."

The penny dropped. Everything Gobby was busy baking in the kitchen was Welsh, or her interpretation of it. There was a massive pile of Welsh cakes; *bara brith*, a traditional Welsh fruit bread; Glamorgan sausages; Welsh cawl, a stew; Welsh rarebit; and *crempog*, or Welsh pancakes. It just went on and on. Dotty even spied a steaming pile of laver bread on the stacked kitchen table: seaweed on toast – yuck!

Dotty was touched, although she really was going to have to tell her that she wasn't a fan of traditional Welsh cooking. Her mother's home baking had been a far cry from Gobby and her kitchen. Dotty's mam could barely boil an egg, let alone make the mountain of Welsh delicacies Gobby had clearly spent some time researching. At the end of the day, they might have lived in Cardiff but Dotty's mother wasn't even Welsh, not that Dotty had known that at the time. Although she was pretty sure her dad was.

Chapter 12

Dotty watched the old woman happily fussing over the table, tidying away the baking tins and making the food presentable. No, Dotty thought. She couldn't tell Gobby that she didn't care for Welsh food. It would break the poor woman's heart. Perhaps she could just let her down gently, starting with the laver bread.

Back Home

Chapter 13

Reunions

Dotty left Gobby happily working in the kitchen and went off to find Great-Uncle Winchester in his study. If he was to be found anywhere in the house, the old man's presence behind his desk was almost as predictable as Gobby's eternal presence in the kitchen.

Dotty gave a cursory knock at the door. "Hi, Winnie." She eyed him nervously, unsure of how he would respond to her. But she needn't have worried.

"My dear girl!" he bounded over and gave her a huge hug. "I've been sick with worry. Terrible business with this illness in school; I wish you'd have let me send a car for you."

"I'm fine, Winnie, truly." It was difficult to be angry with the old man for long.

"Well, that's a relief, I can tell you." The old man ushered her towards the fireplace chairs where they habitually sat. "So fill me in. How many girls have been affected? Have they found out what it is, yet?" He shifted on his seat. "I have to say I'm glad to have you home until this nasty episode has blown over."

"It's affected four girls so far," replied Dotty. "Nobody seems to know what the cause of it is." She paused. "This whole thing, though. I can't help but think…Winnie, you don't think it's because of me, do you?"

Her great-uncle looked surprised. "Darling girl, what a strange notion. Why ever do you think it would it be your fault?"

"With the strange visions I've been having and then – it just feels like whenever I have a new one, that's when more girls seem to be taken sick."

Great-Uncle Winchester smiled at her patiently. "A simple coincidence, my dear. Epidemics always strike in waves, and to you it seems that when it happens, every few days, it is coinciding with your dreams."

"The girls don't think that. They're calling me a witch," said Dotty, biting a nail.

"Girls can be unkind creatures. Now look, my dear, I know this is troubling for you, and your classmates certainly aren't helping, but you have to accept that your dreams are nothing more than a reaction to your recent experiences. Dreams are a great healing tool, you know, helping our subconscious make sense of things we are struggling to deal with in our waking hours."

"But I really do think they are more than just dreams, Winnie. And they are changing: things are happening in them."

"Change might well be expected in this kind of dream, dear girl. That's good – it means your brain is working through things, as I said."

Dotty collected her thoughts, trying to explain herself better. "But I know there's more to it than that, Winnie. There simply must be. The changes: it's like they're taking place in real time. And now it seems that I'm not the only one there. There's someone else in the woods with me."

"Sarah, you mean?"

"No, not Sarah: a third person. Winnie, someone's got into my vision and they're following me!" Dotty fought to keep calm. "In fact, it's worse than that, it's almost as if I'm being watched from all sides."

Dotty's great-uncle gave a knowing nod. "That's a common phenomenon. The feeling of being watched, or even judged. It's just a sign of your anxiety. Please try not to worry yourself over it."

Dotty sighed. "Oh, I expect you're right. I guess the whole thing's just given me the creeps, seeing my schoolmates lying unconscious like that."

Great-Uncle Winchester thought for a moment. "I say, dear girl, do you think you might like to see someone – a counsellor, perhaps? So that you can talk about your dreams: to someone away from home, I mean? A feminine face might be able to put your mind at rest better than I can."

"Thanks, Winnie. That's very thoughtful. But how would I explain who the people in my vision are, or why I feel the way I do about them? And, without the whole truth, how could a counsellor truly help me?"

Dotty's great-uncle looked saddened for a moment. "Of course, that is true my dear. It is difficult for you, I appreciate – I truly do." He smiled. "Then I'm afraid you'll just have to rely on your old uncle for now. But please know that my door is always open, dear girl, if you're ever in need."

"Sure, Winnie."

Discussion over, Great-Uncle Winchester was back to his usual jovial self. "Now, off you run to see Mrs. Gobbins. I believe she has a treat for you."

"Yes, I know, I've already..." Dotty didn't bother finishing her sentence, as she could see that her great-uncle's attention had already returned to his work.

Leaving the room, Dotty harrumphed to herself. Always open. Ha! Always shut, more like. She had hoped to ask her great-uncle about the photograph of her mother, but with all their other talk it seemed she had missed her opportunity. Suddenly feeling at a loose end, she tromped off up to her bedroom. Perhaps she could Skype Sylv. It seemed like ages since they'd spoken.

Sylv was the picture of misery. "So you've made a new friend? That's great." She pouted.

"Oh, Sylv, surely you're not jealous? I thought you wanted me to meet some new people. I bet you've made loads of new friends, too. Although, actually I haven't made loads, just the one," she said, trailing off.

"Well, that's one more than me." Sylv burst into tears. "Oh, Dot, it's awful. I wish I was back at St. Aidan's again…with you."

"Whatever's the matter?" Dotty was worried. Sylv was one of the most happy-go-lucky people she'd ever met. Plus she had a pretty thick skin, much more so than Dotty. It was unlike her to get upset like this.

Sylv blew hard into an oversized hanky: one of her Dad's. "It's these girls, Dot, in year 10. They don't like me. They say I'm fat. They keep calling me 'fatty-la-la'. No one else will talk to me because of it, not even the other girls who came up with me from St. Aidan's. I guess they're afraid of being picked on, too. I hate them."

"That's nonsense, Sylv. You know that. They're just jealous because you're more curvy than they are. Stupid girls. Year 10, you say? They should go and pick on someone their own size."

Dotty felt angry for her friend. Sure, Sylv wasn't the skinniest, but Dotty had never thought of her as fat either. Besides which, she was bubbly and funny and kind, and not deserving of any of this.

"Just take no notice of them, Sylv. They'll soon get bored and go find someone else to pick on."

"Yeah, sure." Sylv gave her nose another blow. "It's just hard, you know? I don't half miss you, Dot."

"Me, too," Dotty admitted. Although hearing about her friend's predicament, she didn't feel quite so bad about hers for now. At least, like Sylv said, she had one friend to look out for her in school. It made a big difference.

"If it makes you feel any better, I'm not so popular myself," Dotty said. "With the exception of Lara, they all think I'm some sort of witch."

"What? Why?" Sylv started. "Unless you've been levitating pencils again," she teased.

"No, nothing like that." Dotty grinned sheepishly. "It's my dreams. I made a fool of myself on the bus on my first day, talking in my sleep, and now they think I'm a bit nuts or something. I dunno." Dotty didn't feel like explaining herself in too much detail right now. She didn't think she would take it too well if Sylv tried to give the situation one of her practical interpretations.

"Look, I know there's a few weeks until half term still, but why don't you ask your dad if you can come visit?" Dotty suggested. "It'd be great to see you."

Sylv beamed. "Thanks, butt, I need something to look forward to, like. I'll go ask him now. Shame my school hasn't closed down like yours has – then I could come sooner."

"Yeah," agreed Dotty. But, in truth, she wouldn't have wished her current situation on anyone.

Reunions

Chapter 14

The Photographs

Not being one to waste time, Dotty hot-footed it straight down to Great-Uncle Winchester's study. "Winnie, can Sylv come and stay with us at half term, please? For the week? Or just a few days if you like?"

Great-Uncle Winchester looked pleased. "Why, yes of course, my dear. Splendid idea. It'll be nice to spend some time with your friend. You invite her up for the week."

"Great, I'll tell her, then."

"And what about you? Have you had any thoughts about what you are going to do when the school re-opens?"

"No, I hadn't thought about it," Dotty replied. "I just assumed you'd want me to go back."

"Dear girl, I'm not an ogre, you know. I know you haven't had the best time of it, what with all the recent calamity. And I would never force you to go if it wasn't what you wanted."

"No, it's fine, Winnie. I want to go back – really." Dotty wasn't a quitter, and she wasn't going to let some nasty bullies get the better of her. Besides, given her increasing suspicions about her own part in causing the illness, in her own mind it would have been too much like leaving a sinking ship if she simply walked out and left them all now.

Great-Uncle Winchester smiled. "That's the spirit, dear girl. And in that case, I have some news for you. I received an email this morning from school. It seems they want you to make use of your time at home in doing a little research. A genealogy project, I believe?"

Dotty brightened. "Oh yes, I've been wanting to speak with you about that. I was hoping you could help me with it."

"Of course, dear girl. Anything." Dotty's great-uncle took of his half-moon glasses and cleaned them on a corner of his waistcoat. "Tell me, what can I do to assist?"

"I need some photos of the family – for a family tree. Do you have some I could take a look at?"

Chapter 14

"Ah, I see." Great-Uncle Winchester looked solemn. "I presume all your family photos were lost in the fire?"

Dotty nodded, feeling a sudden pang of loss. "Sylv's dad dug me out a couple from their album that had Mam and Dad in them, and there are quite a few of me, but they're not the best."

Great-Uncle Winchester nodded. "Well, I have nothing of your father, I'm afraid. Sadly I never had the good fortune to meet the fellow. But I'm sure we will have some of your mother from her younger days if we have a rummage," he said more brightly.

"That'd be great, Winnie, thanks – I'd love that." Dotty paused. "But I was hoping you might have some more family photos, too."

"Like what, dear girl?"

"Like, of you when you were little – and of your father, or your uncle, perhaps? For the family tree."

Great-Uncle Winchester's expression clouded slightly. "An uncle, you say? Well, my dear, I'm not sure what we have exactly, but…"

"Oh, I don't mind rooting through, if you have an old box of photos or something."

Dotty's great-uncle seemed to flounder. "Yes, of course, I'd be delighted to help you in any way I can." He faltered. "It's just that the photos are kept in the family vault. I will need to ask Mr. Strake to bring them up for you when he has a spare moment. Then I can look some out for you."

"As I said, I don't mind looking myself," Dotty persisted. "Perhaps we could do it together."

"Super idea."

Despite his words, Dotty wasn't convinced her great-uncle meant it.

"You will tell him it's urgent, won't you?" Dotty asked. "I can't get on with my genealogy project without them."

"Yes, of course, dear girl. I'll get Mr. Strake onto it straight away."

Dotty left her great-uncle in his study and tromped down the corridor. Ugh! Strake. Dotty loathed her great-uncle's personal secretary. Why did Winnie have to involve him? Strake was odious and greasy and hideously untrustworthy. With that unnaturally curved back of his, he plain gave Dotty the creeps. She hated that she had to rely on him to do anything for her.

And why were the family photos tucked away in the Winchester vault anyway? Was it normal to keep such things hidden away under lock and key in the cellars? Her mam and dad had always kept their photos in a cupboard in the sitting room. Mind you, look what had happened to them. Perhaps a vault was the safest place to put them after all: at least they'd be safe from fire.

Chapter 15

Seeking Answers

Not to be put off in her quest for more information about the elusive Winchester clan, Dotty went in search of Gobby. The old cook had been working in the house since she was a girl, from what Dotty had gathered. She was sure to have some information about Dotty's extended family.

Dotty found her target in the scullery washing up the last of the dishes from her Welsh baking extravaganza. There was a mountain of pots and pans, gleaming and steaming and sparkling in the light from the high windows of the small room. Gobby wiped a soapy forearm across her brow, highlighting it with a trail of suds. Clearly she had been working hard.

"Anything I can help with, Mrs. Gobbins?"

Gobby threw her a tea towel. "You're a welcome sight," she said. "Yes, please, if you wouldn't mind, dear. You can help me with the drying."

They set about drying the dishes together, Gobby stacking them in a neat pile ready to go away in the tall kitchen shelves and cupboards that lined the room. She smiled at Dotty fondly. "My, it's a long time since I had any help in the kitchen."

"How long, Mrs. Gobbins?"

"Do you know, I really can't think." The cook stopped wiping a large copper pan, cradling it in her arms for a moment while she thought. She shrugged. "It feels like forever ago."

"Have you been here a long time, then, Mrs. Gobbins?"

"Yes, dear, since I was a girl – about your age." She picked up an oversized flan dish. "Of course, those days were different than now. The house was full of people, above stairs and under it." A smile played around her lips at the memory. "We had so much work to do – up at the crack of dawn and working till dusk. I was exhausted. Sometimes I used to fall asleep by the kitchen hearth, and my mother would have to carry me up to my bed when she finished her day's work. My, those were happy times, though."

Chapter 15

"So was that when Great-Uncle Winchester's father was alive then? And his mother?"

Gobby paused again, frowning hard, as if with the effort of remembering. "I suppose it must have been." She looked puzzled. "But do you know, I don't remember a time when the master of the house was anyone *but* Mr. Winchester. Well now, isn't that the funniest thing?" She picked up a fresh cloth and started scrubbing a sugar pan with it. "But then, as I told you, I was just a young slip of a thing then. I suppose at my age you begin to forget."

Gosh, thought Dotty. Did people really get to an age where they forget a thing like that? It seemed a bit odd to her, not to mention annoying, as it was one avenue of information she had been relying on. "I was hoping you might be able to tell me a little about them," Dotty explained. "For my school genealogy project. We're making family trees."

"Well, that will be lovely for you, dear." Gobby smiled benignly. "I only wish I could help. I'm afraid you'll have to forgive an old woman her fading memory."

"That's okay," said Dotty. Although in truth she was bitterly disappointed.

Feeling a little less confident but determined to find out something about her family history before the day was up, Dotty decided to call Pip and see if he could shed any light on the matter. She dived into the library – one of her favourite places in the house – and rang the servants' bell to the side of the great stone fire. Perhaps my luck is changing, thought Dotty as Pip came tumbling down the chimney almost straight away and landed with a small thud in the grate.

"At your service, miss." He doffed his cap at her cheekily.

"Hi, Pip. How are you?"

"Mustn't grumble, miss. And yourself? No more troubling dreams, I hope?"

"They're visions, Pip." Dotty snapped irritably. "But that's not what I called you about."

"Oh?"

Dotty shuffled slightly. "I was hoping you could help me with a school project, actually."

"Sorry to say, I've never had much in the way of schooling, miss. But I'll assist in any way I can." He settled himself down cross-legged on the fireside rug. "So fire away, miss."

"We're doing a project about families," said Dotty. "I need to find some old photos of my ancestors. Mr. Winchester has asked that horrible personal secretary of his to dig some out for me."

"I see. An' how can I help?"

"Well, I was hoping you might be able to tell me something about who lived here before Great-Uncle Winchester. About any brothers or sisters he might have had, or about his parents – my great-grandparents."

"Mr. Winchester's father, you say?" Pip removed his cap and scratched his head as he thought about it for a moment. As usual, the blond circle of hair that he hid under his cap was the only clean part of him. "I'm afraid that was before my time, Miss Dotty. Never met a father or a mother. It's always just been Mr. Winchester."

"And how long would you say that was, Pip?"

"Dunno, miss: since I was a scrap. Sorry not to be of more help."

"Oh, that's okay, Pip. I guess I'm just going to have to wait for those old photos from Strake."

With no one left in the house that she could ask, Dotty decided to take a tour of the gardens with Geoff. She had half a mind to ask Kenny the gardener about her great-uncle, but actually he was nowhere to be seen that morning, so Dotty was forced to bring her investigations to a halt, just for the moment.

That didn't stop her mulling things over in her head, of course. Not that there was a great deal to mull, at the present time, as nobody seemed to know anything.

Dotty sighed. She supposed that it was logical that neither Pip nor Gobby should remember a time before Great-Uncle Winchester was head of the household. After all, he was as old as the hills and, she would have guessed, a good fifteen years or more older than the cook. Although, given that she had been there herself since she was a girl, it was a shame she couldn't remember Great-Uncle Winchester's father, or whoever it was that had run the house before him.

As for Pip – well, he was only a boy himself, wasn't he? Although there was that time when he claimed to have known her mother when she was a girl, which, if it were true, made him nothing less than some sort of modern day Peter Pan.

And then there was the photograph at school. Would it really be so unusual for Great-Uncle Winchester to look like his father, though, or even an uncle? After all, people often said Dotty could be mistaken for her mother when she was young. It wasn't so very far-fetched that he should be just like his father then – in eccentric temperament as well as in looks. And as for the name "Great-Uncle Winchester," the teacher could have been mistaken. It could have been "Grandfather Winchester." Even if it wasn't, Winchester was the family name – so weren't they all Winchesters, after all? Anyway, she would find out soon enough Dotty supposed, when she saw the photographs.

Chapter 16

Strake is difficult

By dinnertime there was still no sign of any photos, however, old or otherwise. Dotty wondered if Strake had unearthed them and taken them to Great-Uncle Winchester's office. So off she trotted and there found Strake, but unfortunately Dotty could see no newly-unearthed boxes in his vicinity. When Strake saw Dotty, he heaved an exaggerated sigh, his shoulders shrugging with the effort of making it.

"What is it, Miss Parsons?" he asked in a way that told her he considered both her and her request to be tiresome in the extreme.

"The old photographs I was after; from the cellar. Great-Uncle Winchester said you would look them out for me."

"Yes, Miss Parsons, of course. I had not forgotten, " he said in a tone that suggested he wished he had.

"When do you think you will be able to fetch them?" Dotty asked. "I need them for my school project."

"Miss Parsons," Strake said, putting an emphasis on the "Miss," as if he were using her title as an insult. He stopped writing for a moment, one spidery hand resting on the ledger in which he was making entries. "Mr. Winchester is an important man with a very busy schedule, and I, as his assistant, find myself equally busy doing his bidding. I am afraid your need for diversion is low on my list of priorities."

How dare he? Dotty bit her lip. She knew his slight was intended to upset her, and she wasn't going to give Strake the satisfaction of knowing he had got to her.

"Great-Uncle Winchester assured me that he would tell you to see to it straight away. So clearly it isn't low on *his* list of priorities. So please could you go and fetch them for me? Or shall I go and ask my great-uncle to remind you?"

That did the trick. Dotty smiled as Strake winced at her threat. There was nothing he hated more than being made to look like anything less than his employer's most faithful servant –

especially after his involvement in the plot to steal the Calendar House Key together with the rogue sweep traders, Porguss and Poachling, over a year ago. Dotty still couldn't believe her great-uncle had forgiven Strake for that. She certainly hadn't – and wasn't likely to, for that matter.

"I have to finish these ledger entries, but I will go and retrieve them after supper," he conceded sourly.

"Thank you," said Dotty curtly, and left the room. Finally she was getting somewhere.

Supper came around soon enough, and Dotty couldn't help but feel a little ungrateful as she inwardly groaned to see the tea table positively sagging under the weight of yet another round of Welsh delicacies put on by the matronly Mrs. Gobbins. Dotty picked at a hunk of Welsh rarebit, wishing for the life of her it was good old-fashioned cheese on toast, like her mam used to make.

The fact of the matter was that, despite her kind intentions, Gobby's efforts were misplaced, and Dotty felt that it would be kindest to put a stop to her bouts of Welsh cooking before it got really out of hand.

Dotty looked beyond a steaming pile of Welsh cakes over to the kitchen range, where Gobby was still busy with the skillet. Dotty did hope she wasn't about to hurt the woman's feelings.

"Do you know, Mrs. Gobbins," she ventured.

"Yes, dear?" Gobby paused her endeavours for a moment.

"This is all lovely and I don't want to disrespect Mam and Dad's memory or anything, but - do you know what I've really missed? Your home-baked Yorkshire ham sandwiches."

Gobby's face brightened instantly from one of concern into the absolute picture of joy.

"Well," she said, sounding flustered at the compliment. "As it happens I've just this afternoon cooked a fresh ham." She beamed. "And how about a couple of pickled onions on the side? I've a new batch in the larder."

"That sounds great, Mrs. Gobbins." Thank goodness, thought Dotty: crisis averted.

Gobby bounced over to Dotty and enveloped her in one of her oversized hugs, which Dotty had to admit was pretty heavenly. She melted into the old housekeeper for a moment, breathing her in.

As she came up for air the smell of burning caught her nostrils. "Er, Mrs. Gobbins, I think your Welsh cakes are burning."

Gobby released her charge but, rather unusually in the face of spoiled food, remained all smiles. "No matter," she said, rescuing the charred remains of the Welsh cakes from the range. "They'll do for the dog."

Chapter 16

Crikey! Thought Dotty as the cook waddled off blissfully towards the larder. Gobby must be happy.

After supper Dotty's thoughts returned immediately to the matter of Strake and the photographs. She hadn't thought to ask whether he would bring the photographs to her or whether she should go to his office to collect them, although she supposed that he would probably expect her to seek him out. So after waiting what Dotty considered to be a suitably polite interval of an hour-and-a-half, which felt like an eternity, Dotty made the trip down to his office.

Strake's office adjoined Great-Uncle Winchester's study. Although only marginally smaller than her great-uncle's, Strake habitually kept the door closed and the blinds drawn, which made it feel airless and dull. Not that this came as any surprise to Dotty. She supposed this was simply the way he liked it; and, from her point of view, she wouldn't have been surprised to see him habitually crawling out from underneath a cold, damp rock.

To Dotty's surprise and disappointment, however, when she reached Strake's office it was closed and locked, with no sign of light or movement inside. A quick survey of Great-Uncle Winchester's study door soon told her that he wasn't at home either, leaving Dotty hoping that

Strake hadn't left the photographs inside, before retiring for the night. That would have been just typical of him.

Inclined, rather unusually, to give him the benefit of the doubt, Dotty wondered if perhaps she had been too hasty and Strake was still hunting in the family vault for the elusive photographs, soon to return. Satisfied, for the moment, with her own explanation for his absence, she settled herself down onto the hall rug opposite Strake's office door, her back leaning a mite uncomfortably against the dark oak panelling that cloaked the corridor.

After a 45-minute wait, however she concluded that the horrid snake of a man wasn't planning to return that evening, and that he had probably not been to look for any photographs. Darn it – she should have known not to trust Strake to his word. And it was just so typical of him to be difficult about the task when Dotty's own needs or desires were involved.

Chapter 17

Scant Progress

Fed up and tired of her day's fruitless investigations, Dotty took herself wearily to bed.

As she drifted off to sleep, she prayed that her night would be undisturbed. Sadly, however, Dotty's prayers went unanswered, as that night she had another one of her visions, for the first time since she had been home.

The sense of being watched that had made her so uncomfortable in her previous vision continued, although now it seemed to be intensified. Jarring, it set her teeth on edge. Watching Sarah standing there, just mouthing at her, as if the sound on a telly had broken, Dotty felt like she was the unwilling star of a silent movie and all eyes were on her. Why couldn't they get past this point in the vision? If only she could work out what Sarah was saying, then they could move on. Dotty felt a familiar sense of helplessness and she didn't like it one bit.

In a flash of inspiration Dotty wondered if she could learn how to lip read so that she could work out what Sarah was saying. Perhaps there was a free course or something that she could look up on YouTube. She would get straight onto it, just as soon as she had finished her genealogy homework.

Dotty was actually quite excited about doing her family tree, and so she decided to start mapping it out as soon as she had finished her breakfast. The lack of photos was a problem, of course, but she could always add those later. Sylv had already emailed her over some pictures of herself and her mam and dad. Great-Uncle Winchester had promised to print those out for her. And the old photos from the family vault were sure to be forthcoming shortly. Strake wouldn't dare disobey his master for too long.

But after half an hour of attempting in vain to map out her family tree on various scraps of A4 paper, Dotty began to feel more than a little despondent about her paltry findings.

Chapter 17

Parents?
I
Parents? – (Great) Uncle Winchester
I
Brian Parsons = Gwendoline Parsons (nee Winchester)
I
Dorothea Madelaine Parsons

Dotty's family tree, such as it was, was patchy at best. It was no use. She really did need those photographs, and to glean some more information from her great-uncle, if she could pin him down for long enough.

There was no time like the present, so Dotty trotted off down the corridor, taking a direct route down the main staircase rather than climbing the back stairs, just for a change of scenery. Dotty wished she had her rollerblades on – not for the stairs bit, obviously – but skating around the hallways of the grand house always did make things more interesting. Sadly the pair she had brought with her from Cardiff—one of her only mementoes of her life back in Wales—had grown too small and Dotty couldn't quite bear to replace them.

Arriving at Great-Uncle Winchester's study door, Dotty was pleased to see that he was in residence, although there was still no sign of Strake. Her great-uncle was sitting in his favourite chair by the fireplace, struggling to fit what looked like a pair of crampons to stout leather walking boots.

"Hi, Winnie." Dotty was by now, far too used to her great-uncle's frequent and highly unusual wardrobe changes to be fazed by the scene that confronted her. "Are you planning on going climbing?"

He turned and gave her a gleeful grin. "Adventure, my dear, is the spice of life. You should try a little."

"I have quite enough of that here in the house," Dotty said, smiling back at him. "I just forwarded an email. I wondered if you'd got it yet – it has photos of Mam and Dad on it?"

"Oh yes, of course, darling girl. I have to confess I haven't fired up the old computer yet this morning, but let's have a look."

Great-Uncle Winchester's computer was positively ancient – to the point that Dotty wondered how it still worked. It was big and clunky and housed in a big beige box that jostled for room under his study desk alongside the elderly spaniel, Geoff. Despite that, Dotty had to grudgingly admit that despite its lack of visual appeal, it couldn't be as old as all that because it could send and receive email, and would print almost anything from the equally clunky and ancient-looking printer that was attached to it. The computer hummed loudly as it lumbered into action, like a great beast waking from a lengthy sleep.

Whilst they waited for the computer to boot Dotty took the opportunity to ask after the photos in the vault.

"Has Mr. Strake not brought them up to you yet?" asked her great-uncle.

"No. Actually, I was rather hoping he'd brought them to you, here."

"'Fraid not, dear girl. But I'm sure he's on with it."

Dotty was not so easily reassured. "He said he'd look them out for me last night, but I haven't seen him since."

Great-uncle Winchester fiddled absent-mindedly with the computer mouse. "I have to say I haven't seen him either, my dear." He looked up at her. "I daresay he's probably braving the family vault right now, looking for them."

"That's what I thought last night," mumbled Dotty – more to herself than to her preoccupied uncle. "Well, when you do see him, will you tell him I need them urgently? It's important."

"Yes of course, dear girl. Ah, here it is - the email from your friend. Let me get those printed for you." He smiled at her innocently.

Typical, thought Dotty. She bet anything she wouldn't get the photos before she went back to school.

The printer whirred into action and before long it was chugging out the photographs of

Dotty and her parents taken from Sylv's family photo album.

"Ah," Great-Uncle Winchester said as he took the first one off the printer. "Your father looks like a nice chap. He suited your mother well."

He handed the photo to Dotty and she stared at it, feeling a sudden lump in her throat.

"And here's another one of the three of you. What a super photograph. Taken in your back garden, I assume? My, you do look like your mother."

Dotty looked at the picture. It seemed as if it had been taken in another age: in another existence, long before this one. They were all giggling together – her and Mam and Dad. She remembered the photograph being taken. Sylv had got a new digital camera for her birthday from her mam and had insisted of taking photos of pretty much everything that summer - which was lucky, as it turned out. Sylv had been saying silly things to make them laugh, finally taking the photograph when they all shouted out 'Gorgonzola!' Gosh, Dotty missed those times, and most of all her parents - so much it hurt her physically, like someone had punched her in the tummy – hard.

Great-Uncle Winchester was reminiscing, too, it seemed. He was staring at another photograph taken from the printer: this time of Dotty's mother on her own. "You know, I was so very fond of your mother," he told Dotty sadly. "I really missed her happy face about the place. Until you came along, that is." He smiled at her wistfully.

"What made her leave?" asked Dotty. "Why did she never mention you? Or the Calendar House?"

"I really can't say, dear girl." Great-Uncle Winchester handed her the final photo. "She needed to go off and live her own life: to be herself. To be young, I suppose." He changed the subject abruptly. "Right, that's the last photo, and I'm afraid I have some business to attend to now, my darling, so we'll have to save our chat until later."

"Okay," Dotty knew better than to argue with her great-uncle once he had made up his mind.

"And don't worry," he soothed. "I will chase Mr. Strake with news of the box of photographs from the cellar, just as soon as I see him."

It looked as if Dotty was just going to have to make do with the photos from Sylv for the time being.

Scant Progress

Chapter 18

Sylv has a Plan

A fortnight passed, and finally Wakebury Girls was given the all-clear by the Health Authority, and Great-Uncle Winchester was sent notification that the school was to be re-opened in the week running up to half term. In Dotty's mind, it seemed a bit nonsensical going back just before a break, but at least it meant she wouldn't have to endure it for too long before she was home again, although she would be happy to see Lara, of course. To add to Dotty's frustration and annoyance, there was still no sign of the photos she had been promised, either, despite much chasing of both her great-uncle and his slimy secretary. Still, go she must, though, and so on

Monday morning she found herself back on the train to school.

It was a rather lonelier journey back to Wakebury Girls' than it had been on the way home, as Lara was being driven back to school by her parents. All in all, the experience left Dotty feeling rather low.

To add insult to injury, Dotty's genealogy homework was marked with a 'poor effort' by Mrs. Price. Added to many of the girls' obvious dislike of her, the teacher's ill-concealed disappointment in Dotty's endeavours was a real blow.

"It's not fair," Dotty complained to Sylv during their next Skyping session. "It's not my fault no one will tell me anything, and my family tree seems to be the source of some great unspoken mystery that everyone knows about except me." She moaned. "If Mrs. Price had any idea how hard I tried to get hold of those old photos she might have been less inclined to call it 'poor'. After all, it's not just about some silly project to me – I want to know about my family's history just as much as she does."

Suddenly Sylv gave a wicked little grin. "Don't worry, butt, I've got a plan."

"Really? And what's that?" Dotty raised an eyebrow.

"Never you mind," said Sylv, tapping her nose conspiratorially. "I'll tell you when I see you at the weekend."

Chapter 18

"You really do have a plan?"

"Yes, just you wait and see."

Now Dotty found that the half term couldn't come quickly enough. On the bright side, there had been no fresh cases of 'sleeping sickness', as the girls had dubbed it, so Dotty had to be thankful for that. Perhaps it had just been a virus after all, and nothing to do with Sarah or Dotty or her mysterious heritage.

Nevertheless, Dotty really did hope Sylv had a plan to find out more about Dotty's secretive family, although she couldn't think what such a plan could possibly consist of. Not to be unpleasant, but Sylv wasn't usually the brains of the operation.

Soon enough the eagerly-anticipated break arrived and Dotty, with Gobby as her chauffeur, headed for the local station to collect Sylv. Dotty stood excitedly at the station entrance, waving madly to her best friend through the glass as Sylv fought her way along the station concourse, carrying a huge grey holdall that Dotty suspected belonged to Sylv's dad.

"Hiya, Slyv. Can I help you with that?" Dotty opened the heavy glass doors of the lobby as best she could to ease Sylv's exit from the station.

"Nah, Dot, you're okay. I can manage." Sylv struggled to disentangle the last of the holdall from the doors, which had closed just a little too quickly for her to make a clean exit. Dotty giggled. Sylv could always be relied upon to inadvertently create a humorous situation wherever she went.

Gobby was waiting impatiently for the girls at the station exit in her Citroen 2CV Dolly and waved happily when she saw Sylv, who waved back. "A warning," said Dotty. "She's properly looking forward to seeing you, so she'll probably half smother you to death when she gets the chance. It was all I could do to stop her from going into Welsh-baking-mode again. I had to tell her you wanted to try some traditional Yorkshire food. I don't know what she's cooking up, but I know there are Yorkshire puddings on the menu."

Sylv giggled. "Fine by me, I'm starving."

There wasn't really enough room in the boot of Gobby's Citroen for Sylv's massive bag, so the girls wrestled it into the back seat next to Sylv instead. Dotty sat next to Gobby in front.

As the car sped off along the lanes Dotty craned her neck around to speak to Sylv, mouthing to her as best she could without Gobby overhearing. "So what's the big plan then?"

"What plan?"

"Your plan: the one to find out about my family history."

"You mean the photos?"

"Yes, them." Sylv could be exasperating sometimes.

Sylv gave a wicked little smile. "We're going to steal them!"

Dotty was incredulous. "Seriously? That's your plan? And how exactly do you think we're going to break into the family vault and take what we want without getting caught? Strake keeps the key in his office, for starters. How are we going to get hold of that?"

Sylv was not to be put off. "Oh, we'll find a way," she said, smiling confidently.

Back at the house, the girls had retired to Dotty's room for an early night, citing full bellies and tired eyes as their excuse. This was pretty believable, following a rather-too-large dinner of roast beef and Yorkshire puddings with six different types of vegetable and lashings of gravy, followed by generous slices of rhubarb pie with thick golden custard, and so there was little cause for suspicion. Once there, the girls hid behind the bed curtains, whispering fiercely to one another in true conspiratorial fashion.

Sylv was the first to speak. "Surely we can just wait 'til Strake leaves his office and then sneak in and get it."

"Not likely. He always locks his office door when he leaves for the night. I've never known him not to."

"Okay then, why don't we go to his office together – you can say you need something from him – and while you cause a distraction I'll take the key to the vault. Simple."

Dotty snapped. "It's far from simple. Honestly, your plan just gets stupider and stupider." She didn't want to upset Sylv, especially not right after she arrived, but Dotty was finding it really hard not to show how cross she really was. She had pinned a lot on the idea that Sylv might be able to help her find out more about her family – something she herself had so far failed to do – and it was difficult not to let her disappointment get the better of her.

Sylv looked hurt. "Well, I don't think it's a stupid plan at all. I've thought about it, and I reckon it'll work. Anyway," she insisted, "it's better than the plan you have, which is no plan at all as far as I can see. Stupid or not, I would've thought you'd at least want to give it a go."

Dotty sighed. "I know you're trying to help, but you don't know Strake like I do. The man has the eyes of a hawk. He'll realise something's up straight away."

Sylv retorted. "You forget I've been up close and personal with the guy too, you know. Remember the small matter of the Calendar House Key? You trusted me then. Why not trust me with this? You never know, he might fall for it. I mean, what do you have to lose? All you need is a bit of luck."

Chapter 18

"Famous last words," said Dotty. "But then, hang on a minute – luck. That's it, Sylv. You're a genius!"

"Make your mind up; you were saying I was stupid a minute ago."

"I'm sorry about that, but don't you see? You've cracked it. All we need is a bit of luck!"

The penny dropped. "Awesome." Sylv was all smiles again. "Let's call Pip."

"So you've called me all the way here to ask me to shake your hands, 'ave you? That's not 'ow it's s'posed to work, you know. Sweep's luck is s'posed to be freely given, not requested nor coerced."

"You sound like you're reading out of a text book," Dotty teased. "Look, we're sorry if we've offended you, but it's really important and we thought you could help."

"If I didn't know better, I'd think you two ladies were up to no good," he chided. "Just promise me it's nothing to do with Sarah and them funny dreams you've been 'aving."

"No, Pip, cross my heart." Dotty made a little X on her chest with a forefinger. "It's nothing to do with that."

Pip continued to look sceptical for a moment, but finally relented. "Okay, but you ladies should know luck's a funny thing. It has a mind of its own, you know: as unpredictable as the wind. You don't know what it's going to do or when it's going to change. It's not to be relied upon for a specific result. You understand me? Sweep's luck works on its own. What the fates consider lucky, you might not."

"Message received loud and clear, boss," said Dotty, giving him a mock salute.

"Yes, we understand, Pip," Sylv chimed in, smiling sweetly.

Here we go again, Dotty rolled her eyes at the thought of Sylv and the embarrassing crush she so obviously had on Pip.

"Okay, then." Pip held out a grubby hand. "Who's first?"

Dotty took Pip's hand, and he gave it a firm shake. "Best of luck to you, whatever you's up to," Pip said.

As their hands met Dotty felt a familiar tingle of electricity shoot through her hand and up her arm, leaving her fingertips full of pins and needles, as if she'd been sitting on it for too long. She drew her hand away, balling it into a fist and rubbing it with the other untouched hand.

Slyv looked worried. "It doesn't hurt, does it?" she asked Dotty nervously. She wasn't the best with pain.

"No, it just feels a bit funny, that's all."

Sylv eyed Pip's still outstretched hand, but didn't proffer her own. Instead she smiled at him coyly. "Hey, Pip, isn't blowing a kiss supposed to be lucky, too?"

Dotty sighed audibly. Pip looked first at her and then hesitantly at Sylv. "Well, yes, that is true, Miss Sylvia."

Dotty glared at him. Surely Pip wasn't going to fall for this.

"But apprentisweeps aren't s'posed to. You see I'm, er, not fully qualified to yet."

Sylv laughed. "What training do you need to blow a kiss?"

Pip rankled. "Well, it's the magick what goes with it, you see. It's not as simple as it looks. If it's not quite right the magick might go wrong. It might wear off too quickly, or it just might not work at all."

Dotty was losing her patience. "For goodness sake, Sylv, just take his hand, will you?" she hissed.

Sylv ignored her. "Oh, go on, Pip. Just a little one won't hurt, surely. And by the sounds of it you need the practice." She fluttered her eyelashes. Dotty groaned.

"Seeing as you ask so nicely." Pip quickly blew a kiss along the length of his hand, straight in the direction of Sylv. Then, nimbly avoiding the daggers Dotty was throwing at him with her eyes, he hopped up and away back up the chimney.

What could have turned into another spat between the girls was luckily avoided when the airborne kiss, upon reaching Sylv, somehow caused her to have an immediate and prolonged sneezing fit. This in turn caused Dotty to burst into peals of laughter, amidst plentiful 'told you so's'. Even Sylv couldn't help but see the funny side, once she'd caught her breath.

"I guess you were right, I should have stuck to the handshake," she said, chuckling.

"Could've been worse," said Dotty. "At least Pip wasn't there to witness it."

"Thanks to your Paddington Bear Hard Stare." Sylv blew her nose unceremoniously on a hanky.

"What did it feel like – the kiss?" asked Dotty, suddenly serious.

"It tickled," Sylv replied simply.

Chapter 19

The Family Vault

The girls waited until a quarter to six before going to see Strake. He usually left at six, unless he was settling down for one of his all-too-frequent late night stints at the office, working in the dimmed lamp light until the early hours. Dotty only hoped it wasn't one of those nights.

As Dotty and Sylv neared Strake's office door, Dotty heard raised voices. One was the high-pitched whine of Strake, the other the unforgettable boom of Great-Uncle Winchester. It was clear that he wasn't pleased. This was bad. It hadn't occurred to Dotty that Strake might not be alone. And besides, distracting Strake was going to be a tall order as it was. But a recent altercation with his employer wasn't going to put Strake in the mood to make small talk with Dotty at all – not that he was ever in the mood to make small talk with her.

Dotty motioned to Sylv to hang back for a moment, so that she could listen to the exchange. She couldn't hear much of what Strake was saying, although his apologetic tone was unmistakable. But Great-Uncle Winchester's voice was like a megaphone, and the distance they were from Strake's office she would have struggled not to pick up every word he said.

"Confound it all, Strake. I told you I needed those documents today. Not tomorrow, not Thursday, but today. Now, I am going back to my room to telephone Mrs. McCarthy at the post office, and by the time I get off the phone I want you hammering on her door as if the hounds of hell are at your heels. You will bring me back my package. Do you hear me?"

Amidst more mumbled yes's and apologies, Great-Uncle Winchester strode out of his secretary's office. Quite remarkably, he didn't seem to notice the girls standing in plain view in the corridor as he stormed past and, like a passing typhoon, made the several steps that it took to get from Strake's office door to his own, slamming the great oak door behind him with an almighty crash.

"That was lucky," said Dotty.

"Perhaps we should try again tomorrow," whispered Sylv.

"Hang on a minute – here comes Strake." Dotty motioned for Sylv to duck down behind a conveniently placed suit of armour, whilst a rather harassed-looking Strake exited his room, struggling to do up his top coat as he went. Pulling the door shut behind him, he set off at a rapid pace, almost breaking into a run as he reached the end of the corridor.

"I guess that's that, then," said Dotty. "No chance of talking to him now." She stood up, only half-completing a stretch before another noise caused her to duck down once more. It was something that sounded like the squeak of rusty metal. Sylv grinned.

"What's so funny?" asked Dotty.

"Look behind you."

"No way!" Dotty gawped as the two girls witnessed Strake's office door creak open noisily upon its ancient hinges. In his hurry to leave, Strake mustn't have closed it properly. "I don't believe it. Hey, Sylv, you don't think it's a trap, do you? This just seems a little too easy to me."

"No, butt. I think it's a nice little piece of sweep's luck – just like we ordered," said Sylv, beaming.

Great-Uncle Winchester's voice was still thundering through his study door. "Quick," said Dotty. "Let's go before Winnie gets off the phone."

Not needing to be told twice, Sylv stepped into Strake's room, with Dotty close behind her.

Strake's office couldn't have been more different from his employer's. Everything was neat and ordered, and every drawer labelled. It was a sneak thief's dream. "If the family vault looks anything like this, we should find the photos easily," said Dotty.

On the left hand wall of the office was a bank of keys, each neatly-labelled and numbered in accordance with a plan of the house affixed to the wall beside it. Scanning along the rows of keys, Dotty easily spotted the door to the vault, labelled Room 363 on the plan. Unhooking the key in question she turned to Sylv, "Looks like we're in business."

Now they just had to brave the cellars.

The cellars to the Calendar House were reached via a flight of stone steps leading down from the service corridor. Once at basement level, the girls found themselves looking down a single long, dimly-lit corridor, punctuated by a number of heavy wooden doors. Many of the doors were closed, but those that were open were spilling over with a jumble of furniture and other detritus that Dotty imagined might have once belonged upstairs in the main house. The family vault was a single room sited at the far end of these cellars and guarded by a thick, iron door—a door that remained most definitely shut.

Chapter 19

Armed with torches in case of a power cut, the girls clambered down the stairs and shuffled nervously along the cellar corridor. The damp air was lit by a single bulb, dusty and dim. Sylv was particularly jumpy, and kept asking Dotty whether or not there were rats down there, and whether Dotty had ever encountered one. Dotty somewhat irritably replied that rats were the least of their worries and that, in her experience, she had a lot more to fear from the local bird population than from the odd rodent. That didn't seem to reassure Sylv any, though, and she held on fiercely to Dotty's elbow, jumping at every little noise they encountered in the half light.

Finally, they reached the door that they wanted to open, differentiated from the others by its painted black ironwork. Dotty surveyed the door warily. Although ancient and corroded in places, to Dotty it looked strong enough to hold back a flood, should the need arise. She fumbled around in her pocket for the vault key, hoping that they could rely on Strake's labelling system, and that it was the right one. The key was weighty and solidly made, as one might expect, but otherwise quite unassuming. With an encouraging smile from Sylv and a "go on," she placed the key in the lock and turned it.

Dotty had half expected that the big old key would be too stiff for her to turn without help, but it turned in the lock as easily as a knife cutting through softened butter. Once opened, the door swung out seemingly effortlessly on its great hinges. It must have been recently oiled, she thought.

The contents were rather more of a disappointment, though. Perhaps on account of the orderly state of Strake's office, Dotty had expected to see a highly efficient and rigorously-catalogued vault. But this was not the case. There was evidence of Great-Uncle Winchester's influence all over the room. In short, it was utter chaos. Files lay strewn about everywhere, higgledy-piggledy, and Dotty couldn't see any semblance of order in the piles of papers and documents that lay scattered about.

It was a bit of a blow. Dotty's heart sank as she wondered where to even start looking for boxes of old family photographs. She let out a silent plea to the heavens for guidance. It was going to be like looking for a needle in a haystack.

"What d'you wanna do?" asked Sylv.

"Nothing much we can do, except get searching, I suppose," Dotty replied. "You start at that end and I'll take this. Remember, anything that looks like a box of photos, or an album, will be great."

"Gotcha."

Sylv got straight down to business and started rifling through the pile of papers nearest to her. Usually this would have made Dotty nervous, as Sylv was fearfully messy. But given the haphazard nature of the filing system, if indeed, there was one, she wasn't too concerned – especially when, within a minute-and-a-half, Sylv gave a shout of glee as she uncovered a huge leather-bound volume. "Bingo!" she shouted, waving it about over her head.

"Is it a photo album?" Dotty was stunned.

"Sure looks like it. It's pretty filthy, mind." Sylv blew across the cover as if to prove a point and a cloud of dust filled the air between them.

Dotty coughed. "Well, take a look – is it what we're after?"

"Sure looks like it." Sylv opened the book to the first page, showing Dotty that indeed it was a photo album, although not a particularly recent one, by the looks of it. Still, sure enough, Great-Uncle Winchester stood there larger than life, beaming away through the dust in black and white.

"Is there only one?"

Sylv put the book down and rifled quickly through the box where she had found the volume. But there was no sign of anything else amongst the debris. "Doesn't appear to be anything else with it. No more photos, like."

"Strange," said Dotty. She would have thought there would be hundreds of family photos lurking down here. Still, it was getting very late now. Maybe there were others somewhere, but there was no time to look tonight. For now, the album Sylv had found would certainly make a good start. "Pass it to me," Dotty asked her friend. She was eager to hold it – to touch this newly-discovered relic of her family's past.

"Sure thing, Dot." Sylv tossed the album to her friend a little too clumsily and it landed awkwardly on the floor with a thud, spilling out half a dozen loose photographs from inside the front cover. Tutting, Dotty gathered them up. The photographs were in colour – not black and white like the photos in the album. She caught her breath. And - they were of her mother!

Other than the picture at school, Dotty had never seen any photographs of her mother as a young girl, but her smile was unmistakable, as it was Dotty's own. Pencilled on the back were some notes confirming their contents. One of her mother playing in the gardens simply stated 'Gwennie, Spring '89'. Another was dated 1994 and showed her mother in the kitchen with Mrs. Gobbins in the background looking a little less grey than she did now—although not much. Dotty uttered an involuntary, "Wow."

"Awww, butt. I'm so glad you've found what you wanted. But we'd better get out of here, you know. I'm worrying about us getting caught and, besides, it's pretty creepy down here."

You're right," Dotty said. "And anyway, I can look at the pictures when we get back to my bedroom." Resisting the urge to sit and flick through any more, she left the vault with Sylv and started at a run back to her bedroom, both of them laughing and giggling.

But upon reaching Strake's orderly office, it appeared that their dose of sweeps' luck was about to abruptly run out. For just as Sylv was putting the key to the cellar back onto its hook, Strake appeared like a bad smell at the office door.

"What are you doing?" He gave a vicious little snarl.

Dotty whirled around, hiding the photo album behind her back as best she could, resting it between her and the door jamb as she frantically scanned the corridor for somewhere to hide it.

Quickly, Sylv dived in to the rescue. "Nothing, Mr. Strake," she said, smiling sweetly. "Dotty and me were just checking you was okay, as we noticed your door open."

Strake clearly wasn't taken in by Sylv's little speech, but it drew his attention away from Dotty just long enough for her to slip the album behind a heavy tapestry that hung in the corridor.

"I shall be far better off in the knowledge that you couple of little sneak thieves are well away from my work space," he snapped, his eyes sweeping the girls. Probably looking for evidence of stolen items about their persons, Dotty thought. She clasped her hands innocently in front of her and Sylv twiddled her hair idly.

"Well, as long as you're okay, then," Sylv

answered, still smiling.

Dotty glowered in his direction. The man positively made her skin crawl. "We'll be off."

"Good night," he replied with finality and, letting Sylv slip past him and out of the door, he closed it firmly shut behind them.

Dotty wanted to retrieve the album from behind the drape but something told her not to. She could sense Strake's presence still lurking behind his closed office door, as if he was watching them through it: horrid man. They would just have to go back for it in the morning.

"Phew! That was close," Sylv said breathlessly as they headed back up the corridor and towards Dotty's bedroom.

"You're telling me!" Dotty could feel her heart beating in her chest like a thousand drums. She wished Strake didn't get to her so. No matter. She was just disappointed not to be able to look at those photos tonight. "Looks like our luck ran out, like Pip warned it would," she said.

"Depends which way you look at it," replied Sylv. "After all, we could have been caught."

Chapter 20

Dreaming

Perhaps unsurprisingly, both girls had strange dreams that night as they slept side by side, safely ensconced in Dotty's four poster. Sylv dreamed herself the star of a thrilling detective movie, running through dark, cobweb-filled corridors in search of a secret code book.

Dotty's dreamed of her mother strolling through the gardens of the Calendar House, laughing and smiling with Dotty at her side. But it was interrupted when her mother abruptly vanished and Dotty found herself no longer in a garden, but in a wooded glade – all too familiar but definitely not on the grounds of the Calendar House. She was back in her vision of the Fae.

Dreaming

As Dotty's ears and eyes acclimatised to the darkened atmosphere of the forest, she heard rustling all around her, the woods positively whispering to her, calling her name as she remained quite still in the clearing. But then from in amongst the murmuring din, Dotty felt a more definite presence close to her. It was Sarah.

Dotty stood helplessly, waiting for the hopeless repetition of Sarah's silent calls. But this time it was different. This time when Sarah spoke, Dotty could hear her.

"Dotty," she whispered, her pale face close to Dotty's. "The Key." Sarah's voice was like a radio that needed tuning, drifting in and out of earshot, as if the frequency wasn't quite right. Sarah stayed close, hovering before her in the half light.

"The Key? It was the Calendar House Key that I saw in the strange blue tree then?" Dotty's mind was doing somersaults. "But how did it get there? Doesn't the Vagabond King have it any more?"

"The King was betrayed," whispered Sarah. "My master holds it now." Something crackled, like bad reception, and then Sarah's image began to flicker and fade, only to return a little too sharp – jagged almost.

"Your master?" asked Dotty. "You mean the hob? But what does he want with it?"

"The Fae are collectors of many things: and people and things that are potent alone hold even great power when together."

Sarah's words sounded strange and grown up - not like something a little girl would say at all. Dotty felt as though Sarah was talking in riddles, beginning to sound like one of the Fae themselves. The girl's image started to dim again, to fade out of focus and disappear.

"Sarah, no," Dotty pleaded. "Don't go. Not yet. I need you to tell me more. About the tree – and the locket."

"I must go," replied Sarah. "The magic that brings me to you: it is not safe."

"But the Key," Dotty begged. "I need to get it back, or at least try."

Sarah's face was quite dim now, fading like a memory in Dotty's sleeping brain.

"Help me, Sarah," Dotty called out blindly, the vision almost gone.

"I will lead you to it." Sarah's voice was nothing but a murmur now. "I will lead you to the tree. But we must be careful," her voice echoed as she faded away. "There are Catchers in the woods."

When Dotty came too it was already morning. Her first thoughts were to talk to Sylv, to tell her what had happened. But as she rolled over and reached out to touch Sylv's arm, Dotty already knew that she would be unable to rouse her from sleep. For, as peaceful as she looked, her best friend was sleeping with her eyes wide open.

Dreaming

Chapter 21

Crisis

All Dotty's worst nightmares had just come true. She shook Sylv hard, although she knew her friend would not wake.

A wave of panic started to take over her. "Great-Uncle Winchester," she called out. "Winnie, help!"

Realising that he was most likely too far away to hear her calls, Dotty didn't wait for an answer, but instead ran as fast as her legs would carry her down the back stairs, tripping and twisting her ankle sharply as she slid down the final few steps.

"Ow!"

Gobby, who was busy rolling something out at the kitchen table, dropped her rolling pin in alarm. "My dear, are you all right?"

"Yes, I'll manage. But Sylv isn't. I'm going to get Great-Uncle Winchester."

Without stopping to explain further, Dotty hobbled painfully through the kitchen and darted through the far door in search of her uncle. She soon found him sitting at his study desk, sporting a burgundy quilted smoking jacket and spotted nightcap and looking rather bleary-eyed. Her great-uncle really wasn't a morning person.

"Winnie, come quickly. Sylv's sick."

"Sick?" He looked startled.

"Yes. It's the sleeping sickness. Come on."

The pair dashed back the way Dotty had come, quickly reaching Dotty's bedroom and an already-present and very worried-looking Gobby. "I can't rouse her," she faltered. "She seems to be sleeping with her eyes open."

Great-Uncle Winchester started, and threw a look at Dotty that she couldn't interpret.

"All right, Mrs. Gobbins. I'll see to this, don't you worry yourself."

"Well, if you're sure." The old cook looked less than convinced.

"Yes, I'll call her father and the authorities. You get back to your kitchen. Dorothea, perhaps you would lend me a hand?"

Dotty looked at her great-uncle quizzically. "Yes, of course, Winnie, whatever you need."

With Gobby out of the way Great-Uncle Winchester rounded on Dotty, wearing a frantic expression that shot a bolt of fear through her.

"Why didn't you tell me?"

"Tell you what?"

"That the girls are sleeping with their eyes open."

Dotty felt all at once confused and defensive. "I thought I had." She eyed him suspiciously. "Anyway, why is that important?"

Great-Uncle Winchester sighed deeply. "Because that fact, my dear girl, tells me the cause of your friends' dreamlike state—it is the work of the Dream Catchers."

"Catchers? That's what Sarah said."

"Sarah?"

"Yes. She spoke to me last night in my vision…finally. She said there are Catchers in the woods."

Great-Uncle Winchester looked grave. "I see."

"I was right then. It is magical, this illness. Not a virus, like the school was saying."

"No. Not a virus, dear girl, but something even more perilous. And we must stop it in its tracks if we can—before it spreads so far we can no longer contain it."

A sudden realisation struck Dotty like a heavy blow to the chest. "Oh, my goodness," she moaned, slumping down on the bed next to her friend. "If the Catchers are using my visions to escape into the dreams of sleeping children, that means the sleeping sickness *is* all my fault. If it wasn't for my visions, they would never have come, and now Sylv taking ill is the final proof."

Great-Uncle Winchester took Dotty by the shoulders and looked her squarely in the face. "This is not of your doing. You have to stay strong for your friend. Stay here with her. Phone her father for me. Let him know she has succumbed to the mystery illness that's been going round the school. I must go to the Council at once."

Dotty turned to Sylv, staring sightlessly at the dark green canopy of the bed Dotty had always seen as a safe haven since her arrival at the Calendar House.

"Please wake up, Sylv," she pleaded silently. "For me?"

But her best friend did not wake.

Later that afternoon Dotty and Pip sat in silence on the edge of her bed. It felt so very empty without Sylv in it. The ambulance crew had come some while ago and taken her to the hospital. Dotty was dubious as to what the doctors could do. Great-Uncle Winchester, much to her annoyance and frustration, had done another of his disappearing acts (he really did choose the worst times to do that – sometimes Dotty thought he did it on purpose). But Pip, who thankfully, was there, reassured Dotty that at the very least, the hospital would be able to take care of Sylv's sleeping body, making sure she had nourishment and any other care that she needed until she awoke.

Sylv's dad was holding vigil at her bedside, having promised Dotty that he would call if there was any change. Although given the nature of Sylv's condition, Dotty knew that she was more likely to be in the know about any change in her wellbeing than her father or the medical staff at Wakebury General.

Pip gave Dotty's hand a comforting squeeze. "Try not to worry, miss. We'll find a way. Just you wait and see." He gave her a bleak smile that was more of a grimace, and less than encouraging.

Dotty sighed irritably. "So tell me. What are they, these Catchers? And where do they come from?"

Pip looked solemnly at her. "The Dream Catchers are ancient spirit folk, born of the forests of the Fae and living in the shadows of the spirit realm. If you like, they are a sort of by-product of the magic created by the faerie folk of the old world. The Fae saw them as a blemish on their world, so they cast them out, not really paying mind to where they went. Their only concern was that they were outside the Fae, of course. But the Dream Catchers managed to survive, eking out a sort of half-life in the space between the Fae and the world of men. They are sustained by feeding off the imaginations of the innocent wherever a chance presents itself. And at a terrible price."

"What price?" Dotty asked, her voice a hoarse whisper.

"The Dream Catchers must keep on feeding to stay alive. They will keep their victims in a dream-like state indefinitely, unless they are stopped."

Dotty gasped. "And by the innocent you mean children?"

"Yes, miss," replied Pip gravely.

"They're nothing but monsters!" Dotty exclaimed. "Can they be stopped? Can't Sylv and the other girls be woken? Is there not a counter spell or something that can jolt them out of sleep?"

Pip shook his head. "Once the Dream Catchers latch on to an innocent mind they won't give it up without a fight. It would take the strongest of magicks to rouse a child from the sleep of the Catchers. And even then you would risk waking their bodies but leaving their minds behind with the spirits that hold them. It's just too dangerous."

Dotty was aghast. "But Pip, that's terrible! Surely there's something the Sweep's Council can do?"

"Well, miss, that's exactly what Mr. Winchester is trying to find out."

Twenty-four hours passed and still there was no news on Sylv and the other girls' conditions, either from the hospital or from Great-Uncle Winchester and the Sweeps' Council. Pip told Dotty to sit tight, but Dotty was not one for waiting to see how things panned out. She wanted to take action, or at least to see action being taken. Knowledge is power, Dotty's Dad had always told her, admittedly usually when he was admonishing her for not learning her spellings, so she decided to start by looking for answers in the library. There simply must be something about Dream Catchers and how to get rid of them in there.

Soon she was surrounded by a significant number of discarded volumes that lay strewn on the floor around her. She was reading a book on folklore and was immersed in a section on "Wisps and Other Wood-Dwelling Spirits", when she caught sight of her great-uncle standing in the doorway. She flung the book to the floor along with the others, and greeted him with an expression that was a mixture of thinly-veiled accusation and disgust.

"What do you want?"

"I don't think you'll find anything on the Catchers in there," he ventured.

"Let me guess, you have a secret stash of books in your study with all the useful stuff in it."

"Well, as a matter of fact…"

"Oh, for goodness' sake. You might as well tell me. You obviously know all about them." She complained.

"What would you like to know?"

"Well, Pip told me a bit. That these creatures, these Dream Catchers, are spirits that feed off the dreams of innocent children to survive. But I don't understand how they got into my vision. And why aren't they feeding off me? Why the others?"

Great-Uncle Winchester smiled patiently at her. "Because, as you said yourself, you have never truly been dreaming – you're communicating directly with the spirits. The visions you've been having. They are an opening: a portal to the Fae, opened by Sarah, using magick that she can't properly control."

"Okay. And what about the other girls?"

"They are less lucky. Once the Catchers have found their way into the Fae, from there they are free to travel into any unconscious mind they find close to hand."

"Which is why whenever I have a vision, people close to me are being affected."

"Yes. That's what we think."

"And what about Sarah. Is she safe?"

"Yes, they will not harm her. She is simply part of the spirit world in which they now reside."

Dotty paused for a moment, taking it all in. "Okay, assuming I follow that, which I don't quite, that still doesn't explain how the dream catchers entered the Fae in the first place; or how we get rid of them, for that matter."

Her great-uncle replied, "Think of it like this. By reaching out to you, Sarah has made a rip in the curtain that separates the world of the Fae from the world of Men. Things like that – they can be sensed by magical folk. Someone's noticed the tear in that curtain and they are using it to their advantage. Whoever it is that's watching, they've opened that chink in the veil to peek through, and they've let the Dream Catchers in."

"So I was right. Someone is watching me then: spying on me in my visions." Dotty gave an involuntary shudder. "And this person: have they let the Catchers in on purpose, or by accident?"

Great-Uncle Winchester gave a small shrug. "It's difficult to say, my dear. Although I can't see why anyone would purposely want to unleash them on the innocent. Either way, they need to be stopped."

"And how do we do that?"

"They need to be called back to the fire. We must set a trap for them. But ancient beings require an ancient spell. That is beyond the sweeps' magicks."

"But you will find a way? You and the Council?"

"The Council will help if they can, yes."

Winchester's response made Dotty angry. "Sounds like a pretty half-hearted attempt to me," she spat. "Tell me, why is that? Do they not consider the Ordinary Folk worthy of help?"

"Darling girl, I am a guardian to the sweep world, not to the land of the Fae or to the world of men. The Council and I together - we will do our best, but our responsibility lies with the sweeps, not elsewhere."

"That sounds like a pretty poor excuse from where I'm standing," said Dotty.

"Dorothea, you are young and impetuous and there is much you do not understand."

"Only because you won't tell me!"

Great-Uncle Winchester smiled patiently. "I appreciate your frustration and perhaps I'm being too protective of you. But you must understand, we've only just found each other and I'm so very keen not to lose you."

"How is giving me the information I keep asking for going to lose me? You're more likely to lose me by keeping me in the dark like you are doing – let me tell you that."

"Yes, I'm beginning to see that." He smiled. "My, you really are a Winchester."

"I'm not sure whether to take that as a compliment or not."

"Oh, you should definitely take it as a compliment, dear girl."

The pair allowed each other the briefest of smiles.

"Anyway, my dear, I fear you have been a little too quick in making your judgments today, for the Council have already sent out scouts to find out what is the cause of this mess, and I can assure you they will be back with answers before long."

"I just wish they'd done something sooner, Winnie. Then Sylv might not be in the hospital now."

"Yes, I know, my dear. But they are doing something now, and under the circumstances we can't ask any more of them than that."

Perhaps Dotty's great-uncle had a point. Or maybe it was just the fact that she had a plan of her own that made her so accepting of his reasoning. For tonight Dotty was going to do something she hadn't dared try before. She was going to see if she could influence her vision – and in the process catch whoever followed her.

Crisis

Chapter 22

Pieces of the Puzzle

Despite Dotty's plans to influence her vision, it was becoming increasingly difficult to push aside her fear of them, now that she knew the effect they had on those around her. Even though Great-Uncle Winchester had assured her that the Dream Catchers could not harm Dotty in any way, and despite the fact that there was no other child in the house that could possibly be affected by the magical plague that she seemed to bring back with her after every vision, Dotty now viewed her exchanges with Sarah as dangerous and unstable. Quite simply she didn't want to be responsible for any more injury – whether to herself or to others.

Gobby clearly sensed Dotty's unease because after supper she offered to sleep in Dotty's room with her. "Just for tonight, dear."

Dotty tried to refuse, but once Gobby had an idea in her head there was no shifting it. So before Dotty knew it Gobby had set up a little camp bed next to the four-poster and was settling herself down in her voluminous nightgown and matching frilly nightcap. "Now don't fret, dear," she chattered. "I'll be right here with you, so don't you worry yourself about any bad dreams." Then, settling her head down on the pillow, she fell instantly into a deep sleep that Dotty was pretty sure even the dead couldn't wake.

Dotty watched Gobby sleeping for a minute or two, and it occurred to her as she gazed at the old cook's freshly-scrubbed rosy cheeks that she didn't ever think she'd seen her minus a covering of flour. She smiled to herself and turned over, punching the pillow into submission in a bid to get comfortable and join her roommate in sleep.

Sleep was not as quick to claim Dotty though. She tossed and turned, worrying that if she slept somehow Gobby might be affected, even though she knew that the Dream Catchers only targeted children. As far as anyone knew, that was. But then, there was always a first time, wasn't there? That said, it was difficult for her to fight sleep when she was so deprived of it. The culmination of quite a number of sleepless nights ensured that Dotty finally fell into a deep and dreamless slumber.

As usual, this was not the case for long. Dotty's eyes fluttered open and she found herself once again in the forest, with Sarah beckoning her to follow. Dotty followed Sarah willingly for the moment, running quickly through the woodland to keep up with her guide. But tonight Dotty had her own agenda. She wanted to discover who was pursuing her. As they reached the clearing, rather than carrying straight on through the forest glade and following Sarah deeper into the woods, she stopped without warning and turned to face back the way she had come.

Suddenly face to face with her stalker, what she saw made her start so violently that she broke from her vision and found herself unceremoniously ejected from the Fae and back into her bed. Tearful and breathless, Dotty fought to take in what she had witnessed: for the being that followed her wasn't a person, as she had assumed it would be. It was a giant magpie.

Dotty sat bolt upright in bed, panting. Although she had only seen it for a second, the image of the bird's beady eyes staring at her with malevolence, burned into her mind like a white-hot brand. Dotty screamed.

Gobby was up like a rocket, quickly tending to the terrified Dotty, shushing her quietly and smoothing her brow.

"There now, poppet: everything's fine. It's just a dream. You just take a breath or two. That's it."

"Something was following me, Mrs. Gobbins. It was a bird – a huge bird."

"You really don't like birds, do you?" Gobby looked at Dotty with concern. "Now then, you listen to me. No bird can harm you. Mark my words – not with your old friend Mrs. Gobbins to look out for you." She smiled. Then, smoothing Dotty's brow one last time, she headed for the kitchen with promises of a cup of hot cocoa to help Dotty to get back to sleep.

Once alone, Dotty's mind reeled. Was she right to think that it was a magpie she had seen? Was it another of the Vagabond King's henchmen? She thought so, but it couldn't be Mordecai. He was blind, after all, not to mention so tattered and dirty you could hardly see the white of his feathers at all amongst the dirt. So there must be another. Dotty had assumed Mordecai was one of a kind, but perhaps there were more of them.

Whoever – or whatever – it was, at least Dotty knew who was following her now. She would go straight to Great-Uncle Winchester in the morning and they could get to work finding the hateful creature. Oh, how Dotty hated birds with their flappy wings and their beady little eyes. To think she had begged Mam and Dad for a budgie when she was younger. And thank goodness they had said no!

But for once, when morning came there was no need for Dotty to go in search for her great-uncle, as at first light the old man was busily knocking on her bedroom door, asking for an audience.

"Dorothea," he called, battering on her door quite unceremoniously. "Dear girl, do open up. I have news."

Dotty leapt out of bed and opened the door for him, ushering him in without further ado. "Whatever is the matter, Winnie?"

He eyed the empty cot bed and then the room, cautiously.

"It's okay, Winnie, she's gone. Got up an hour ago to make the breakfast, she said."

Great-Uncle Winchester looked relieved.

"So what is it?" Dotty pressed him. "I hope nothing else bad has happened."

"No, darling girl, not at all – nothing like that." He paced the room in his carpet slippers, his nightgown billowing around his legs as he did so. "It's just that I have heard back from the Council's scouts and I thought you would want to hear straight away."

Dotty leaned forward eagerly, tucking her tousled hair back behind her ears as if to better hear the news. "Yes, of course. What did they say?"

"A couple of scouts had made their way to an old fairground. The traditional kind – you know, with merry-go-rounds and coconut shies and all that sort of thing."

"Yes, yes." Dotty was impatient.

"Well, those sorts of places are often a good source of information. Many of the folk that run the fairs still practice the old ways, keeping their connections with the Fae alive."

"Okay. So what did they find out?"

Great-Uncle Winchester leaned towards her conspiratorially. "The scouts were planning on visiting an old crone by the name of Orla. She has for many years been blind but plies a trade telling fortunes at the fair, keeping her ear to the ground for news from the spirit world. She usually has a good idea of what is going on in the Fae.

"But before they had a chance to announce themselves, they overheard a conversation that was taking place. Well, they're not so sure it was a conversation going on in the fortune teller's tent, so much as the old woman boasting to herself – they never heard another voice in response to hers. Either way she was very pleased: congratulating herself on the wonderful bargain she had made—a bargain in exchange for a potion."

"What kind of potion?" asked Dotty. "What does it do?"

"It's complicated. But to cut a long story short, it allows its user to enter the Fae."

Dotty gasped.

"But that's not the most interesting part," Great-Uncle Winchester continued. "What is really interesting is what she received in exchange for the potion."

"What, what?"

"Her sight - by virtue of a mechanical eye."

Dotty shrieked. "Mordecai! I knew it. Except, well, I didn't really. I didn't think it could be him."

"Darling girl?"

"I saw him, you see. Last night – in my vision. He was the one following me in the woods. Except it can't have been him. This bird was young and strong – quite beautiful, really. Not like that grimy old bird. And anyway, he could see."

Dotty's great-uncle gave her a patient look. "That doesn't mean it wasn't him."

"That makes no sense," Dotty said.

"I know," Winnie replied. "But you have to remember that in the Fae things do not exist in their earthly form. The appearance they take is dictated by the rules of the Fae Folk." Great-Uncle Winchester paused for a moment. "Take Sarah, for example. In the world of the Fae, all her worldly woes are gone – her legs no longer brittle and bent, her breath is easy, her hunger is quenched. It would be the same for the bird."

"So outwardly, Mordecai would be transformed into the best version of himself whilst he is there?"

"Quite, dear girl."

"And yet I didn't change much at all."

Dotty's great-uncle smiled at her.

"But anyway, even if it was Mordecai I saw in the woods, what does he, or the Vagabond King, want with me? They already took the Calendar House Key. What else could they possibly want? And why would they release the Catchers into the woods?"

"That we can't say for sure, my dear. You said you saw the Calendar House Key in the woods. Perhaps the Vagabond King lost it somehow, and now he wants it back." Great-Uncle Winchester sat down heavily on the bedside chair, causing it to groan under his great weight. "As for the Dream Catchers, all the bargain tells us is that he is in league with the fortune teller. The scouts heard no mention made of Dream Catchers or what their part in all this might be, if at all. It is my personal contention that the Catchers were allowed in by mistake: a magical error that allowed them to slip through the veil when Mordecai opened the portal into the Fae."

"I see."

Her great-uncle continued. "Whatever he is there for, it must be important. After all, the Vagabond King has made a bargain with the crone to exchange a potion for the mechanical eye belonging to his henchman."

"That seems a very odd thing to do – unless he and Mordecai have fallen out."

"That is one presumption we could make, my dear. Yes."

"But then, why would Mordecai help the Vagabond King to retrieve the Key?" Dotty's mind was racing with thoughts and possibilities.

"Perhaps the Vagabond King has a greater hold over him. Perhaps Mordecai was somehow responsible for losing the Key and he needs to make amends."

"I would say losing his eye was amends enough," Dotty exclaimed.

"Perhaps he thinks he will get it back if he appeases the King," mused Great-Uncle Winchester.

"Unless Mordecai does not know his eye has been given away, of course." Now if that were true… An idea began to form in Dotty's mind.

"So now to draw out the catchers." Great-Uncle Winchester interrupted Dotty's chain of thought. "Now we know what we are dealing with, I think they can be quite easily drawn." He continued. "Although we'll need another potion from our friendly fortune-teller to open the portal again. The more difficult part is who we can send into the Fae to do the job. The risks are great – anyone who goes in could be trapped on the other side indefinitely."

Dotty paused for a moment, framing her thoughts. "What about sending in somebody who already knows their way around?"

"It's too dangerous, darling girl. I couldn't let you go."

"I didn't mean me," said Dotty, with a smile. "I meant Mordecai."

Chapter 23

Kings and Castles

Dotty was wearing her determined face. "I'm going to go and see him. And don't say I can't go, because I shall anyway."

"That's out of the question. Raven's Fall is too dangerous. You won't be safe," said Great-Uncle Winchester.

"You didn't mind me going into the Tanneries to meet with the Vagabond King, when he kidnapped Joe."

"Dear girl, that was different. You met at his invitation; his demand, even. You didn't just barge in on him at his secret hideout. And besides, Pip was with you."

Dotty rolled her eyes. "Pip may have been watching me, but he wasn't with me. Not in the

way you're making out. And anyway, the bird
won't hurt me."

"What makes you so sure?"

"Because I'm going to tell him where to find
his precious eye."

Dotty had to rise early the following day to catch
the bus that would take her to her destination. It
was almost a full day's journey by bus to the place
that Mordecai made his home, and Dotty was
tired when she reached the small inn that sat
closest to the ancient moorland that housed the
castle ruins known as Raven's Fall. Apparently
Great-Uncle Winchester was an old acquaintance
of the owner of the Grateful Dragon, and Pip had
gone on ahead and made the arrangements. One
of the blessings of chimney travel, and something
Dotty sorely missed, was the ability to arrive
anywhere in an instant.

The Grateful Dragon wasn't the best-kept of
public houses, not that Dotty was particularly
well-acquainted with any others, but the weeds
growing out of the gutters and the peeling
paintwork didn't make for the best impression,
even to an eleven-year-old girl. Dotty peered up
at the dirty signboard that creaked above her in
the breeze. It pictured a rather sorrowful-looking
dragon shaking hands with a knight in a suit of
armour. He must have been pretty desperate to
want to stay here, Dotty thought. The landlord
was jovial enough though and she could see how

he and Great-Uncle Winchester would get along. On seeing Dotty the landlord quickly ushered her through a surprisingly busy public bar into a modest but comfortable room: away the prying eyes of anyone who might question why a young girl should be travelling alone to a remote inn on the edge of the heath.

Pip greeted her in his usual enthusiastic manner, and once orders had been made for hot chocolate—with all the trimmings, please—and a large plate of biscuits, as Dotty was starving, the pair got straight down to business. Dotty had been insistent that any sign of sweeps was sure to spook the bird, and so it had been agreed that Pip should escort Dotty to the edge of the moor only, returning to the inn to wait for her there once his job was done.

"Are you sure I can't persuade you to let me escort you the whole way to the castle, miss?" Pip asked, his face showing that he already knew the answer to his question.

"No, Pip. It's best I go alone." Dotty squeezed his arm. "Don't worry – I'll be fine. And I know you'll be right here if I need you, okay?"

"Right you are, miss." Pip gave her a resigned smile. "But let me at least give you this – just in case." He held out a handful of what looked like small, burned-out matches.

Dotty eyed them suspiciously. "And they are?"

"Just a little bit of sweep's help, is all. How else are you going to let me know if you need me?" he replied.

Dotty smiled. "Good to know you've got my back, Pip." She shoved the sticks in her pocket. "Well I suppose we'd better get on with it, hadn't we?"

It was only a short trip down the lane to the edge of the moorland, and the start of the track was clearly defined, which gave Dotty a little bit of comfort; although it quickly wound off and out of sight and she wished she could see a little farther in. She didn't like the idea of being lost and alone on the heath with a bunch of scary big birds on the loose.

"Now then," Pip said, interrupting her thoughts. "You follow the track by the side of the stream for about half a mile and then take the right hand fork away from the water, under a disused railway bridge, and carry on the smaller path until you get to the ruin. The last bit's quite a steep climb, so don't be put off by that. You won't see Raven's Fall until you're upon it as it's pretty overgrown at the bottom." He gave her a rare hug that took Dotty by surprise. "Good luck, Miss Dotty."

Dotty hugged him back, not wanting to let go. She wished she could take him with her to the castle, but she knew she had a better chance talking to the Vagabond King's henchman without a sweep by her side. Finally, but altogether too soon for Dotty, Pip released her and took a step back, setting her free. It was time.

It was fine enough weather and would have been a pleasant walk if Dotty had not been so nervous about the meeting ahead. Her stomach felt like it was tied up in knots. She shouldn't have eaten all those biscuits. Pip's directions were good though, and sure enough after fifteen minutes or so she saw a fork in the path. The left fork followed the line of the stream as it meandered through the lower ground, whilst its narrower counterpart veered off to the right, starting to climb as it petered out in the distance. All Dotty's instincts told her to go left and follow the more well-trodden path, but she knew her destination lay to the right. So up the rocky track she trudged, feeling her confidence ebbing from her as she went.

Only a few hundred feet further onto the moor, Dotty saw an overgrown railway bridge lying out of reach of the sunlight. Ivy clung to the crumbling red arch, forcing the pointing from between the bricks. Looking at it, Dotty wasn't entirely sure that a path lay beyond it at all. Had Pip really meant her to go under the bridge, or to simply pass by it? No, he had definitely told her to go under it. As Dotty walked towards it she got a sense that the opening signified the entrance to another place entirely. The air about it whispered; it felt somehow different, even foreboding. Dotty didn't like it one bit.

At first Dotty found it hard to see a trail at all. But as she fought her way through the underbrush she could see that there was indeed a line of travel of sorts. She wondered how long it was since it had been traversed by human feet. As she battled up the steep incline she kept her eyes peeled for the sight of a ruined castle – a large romantic ruin looming against the skyline. But none came and after a time, as the land began to level and the path widened out again, Dotty thought she must have missed it. At the top of the hill the path merged with what she assumed must once have been an old dirt road or cart track, with a high hedge to the right and the heath land falling away to the left. There she paused for a moment, considering what to do.

But a sudden movement up above caught her eye, forcing her to look up. It was a bird with black plumage, standing atop a high stone wall that protruded beyond the hedge line. The bird peered at her with beetle-y little eyes, and Dotty noticed that it had red legs and a red beak – not yellow or grey as one might have expected. Dotty recognised it as a chough: an ancient breed, part of the crow family, but very rare in England now. She had seen one on a family holiday to West Wales once when she was quite young. Her dad had gone on and on about it. Strange to see a bird like that in these parts.

It darted through a fissure in the stonework and out again and, as it did so, Dotty realised this was not just a stone wall, but part of a much larger structure. She had found Raven's Fall!

As the discovery dawned on her the little chough sounded the alarm. "Intruder. Intruder!" it shrieked, hopping from one red leg to another. And before Dotty could speak or bid it be quiet what seemed like a thousand other birds rose from the parapets like a malevolent cloud, shrieking and calling their alarm. "Master, we are found. A human walks among us!"

Dotty half-ran, half-walked a few more paces along the track, rounding the corner of the building, only to see a vast stone structure rising up out of the ground. The building would once have been magnificent. But Dotty could not appreciate the architecture as a whole, because she was too transfixed by the stonework, which seemed alive: moving with the birds that clung to it and crawled across its ancient stones. Their nests squeezed into every nook and crevice, and a thousand eyes from a hundred different breeds of bird, from common blackbirds to crows, rooks, and the rare chough that had sounded the alarm, all watched her every movement.

And at their very heart, in the roofless room that had once been the castle's great hall, before an open fire, stood a bird Dotty both recognised and feared beyond all others. His clouded sightless eyes did not turn towards her but, signalling the smaller birds to hush with a swipe of his wing, he hailed her.

"Greetings, Mistress. I would say it be good to see you, but of course…." He gestured towards his blind eyes.

"Mordecai," Dotty whispered. She could hardly believe this to be the same bird that had followed her in her visions. He stood filthy and ragged, his gnarled talons torn and scarred, red from some recent injury; his dirty feathers so grimy that the white of them was scarcely decipherable from the black. And then, of course, there were those terrible, unseeing eyes.

"That is indeed me name," he replied. "And yet I do not remember inviting ye to use it. Nor do I remember ye requesting my permission to trespass upon me land."

The birds were still, all eyes upon her. There was a heavy silence. Suddenly Dotty was hit with the realisation that this might not be the easy discussion she had hoped for, and it was terrifying. Feeling that her mouth was dry, she took a moment to clear her throat.

"Nor do I remember inviting you into my visions," she retorted.

The bird inclined his head. "And what visions would those be, young miss?"

"Mordecai, sir, there is no time for games. I would speak with you about the forest of the Fae as a matter of urgency." Dotty pushed on. "Many lives are in danger, and if you do not help, I fear that many more will be at risk."

"Ye are wanting me help?" The bird squawked a laugh. "And tell me, girl, why on God's green earth would I want to help the likes of ye?"

"Because," she began, "it is your fault they are at risk."

"Ha! I did not know this were to be a comedy, young lady."

All the birds around him tittered. Darn it. Dotty was losing her audience. She could not afford to get this wrong.

"She has nothing!" screeched the chough.

Dotty was beginning to lose her cool. "It's no joke! You have a responsibility to them."

"Pah!" the bird spat. His brethren fidgeted on their stony perches.

Dotty tried again. Surely this bird was not completely without a moral compass? "The Dream Catchers were unleashed by you when you opened the portal into the Fae and followed me into it. Don't you understand? You let them in, too. Now they are free to wonder in the forest of the Fae and claim the sleeping souls of the innocent. They take fresh victims with each new day. You have to help us bring them back, Mordecai. You just have to."

The great bird took a step towards Dotty, measured and precise. He bent his head just a little, which put his beak in line with her mouth, and spoke slowly and deliberately. Dotty could smell his last meal on his breath.

"So ye say I have let these Catchers in. But why should I care what they do? I have no interest in the troubles of the ordinary folk. Me only concern is with me own brethren – those that ye see here."

"And in following your master's orders," Dotty snapped at him bitterly.

The bird ruffled his feathers indignantly. "I owe him a debt."

"Yes, I've seen it. Hanging from a tree in the land of the Fae. Tell me, Mordecai: how exactly did you lose the Calendar House Key?"

A cry went up amongst the birds. Was that surprise that Dotty heard?

Mordecai waved her question away. "It matters not," he argued. "All that matters is that ye no longer have it."

"You are right," she faltered. Heavens – nothing seemed to be shaking this confounded bird. Dotty knew that she had only one argument left now. She only hoped it would work.

"But there is something that I think will matter to you," she said. "Information I will trade in return for your help."

"And pray, what is that, missy?"

Dotty took a deep breath. "Information about your eye."

At this a cacophony of shrieks, squawks, and screeches filled the air as the birds rose up indignantly at the mention of their master's lost eye. But with another sweep of a tattered wing, Mordecai silenced his feathery cohort. "Tell me," he said.

"Only if you promise to help catch the Dream Catchers."

"Okay, ye have me word."

Dotty searched his cold, unmoving features for some sign of emotion: some meaning. She wondered if it was a promise he would keep.

There was one last thing she needed to ask. "And also to return the Calendar House Key to the Sweep's Council."

"Ye ask me to betray me Master?"

"You owe the Vagabond King nothing. He has betrayed you. He told you he would give you back your eye if you retrieved the Calendar House Key, didn't he? Well, he lied. He has no intention of returning it to you." Dotty stood her ground. "He's already given it to somebody else. A gypsy woman by the name of Orla: the same woman who gave you the potion to enter the Fae."

At her words, the birds screamed and danced in a furious uproar and this time Mordecai did nothing to silence them. Dotty was terrified. She didn't know if he was more angry at his master for betraying him or at her for bringing him the news. Suddenly she felt very small indeed.

When the commotion subsided a little Mordecai finally spoke. "And what makes ye think I would believe this to be true above what me Master tells me?"

"Just check," Dotty replied, pulling herself together. "Send one of your birds to the fairground. You will see that she has it."

Mordecai took a moment, drawing himself up to his full height in front of Dotty. At that moment, he seemed truly terrifying.

"Supposing yer story be true," he started. "How do ye propose we catch these spirits?"

"We will get another spell from the crone that holds your eye. When next you enter the Fae, the Catchers will recognise the portal as the one through which they entered and will be drawn to it. But it is a trap. As soon as they have all entered the portal we will close it, and them along with it."

"Ingenious," the bird cackled. "And your part in this?"

"I will stay and close the portal. There is no need for me to come back into the Fae with you—assuming you know the way."

Mordecai smiled. "Oh, indeed, I know the way, missy. Thanking ye kindly. And in that case, it seems I have an appointment with a crone to keep. Stoneye, Stalefoot, attend me," he ordered two large ravens who immediately took their place at his side. "You will be my eyes – for the journey there, at least." Then he inclined his head toward the rest of the birds, "Me brethren," and with one great flap of his wings he and his raven escort lifted up into the sky and were gone.

Dotty looked around her, realising she was now alone in the middle of a crowd of very unfriendly-looking birds. The assembly chattered with glee, hopping from foot to foot, and Dotty suddenly felt uncomfortable indeed, and very much alone. Putting on her bravest voice, she said, "Please let me pass."

The small red-legged chough advanced a pace. "Oh, I don't think so, missy."

Dotty looked on in alarm. "You wouldn't harm me. After everything I've just done. I came to help your master!"

The chough cackled. "And he thanked ye kindly for it." He leered at her. "But ye came to make a bargain with Mordecai the Eyeless, not with us." He motioned to the assembled birds. "So now that he is gone the question really is, missy, what can ye offer *us* in return for your safety?"

"Well, I…" Dotty faltered. She hadn't anticipated this. She reached into her pocket. What could she offer them? Feeling around with her fingertips she touched the charred sticks Pip had given her. "I have these." Without taking her eyes off the bird, slowly Dotty removed her hand from her pocket, cupping the sticks carefully in her palm.

The chough scampered forwards to have a look at her offering. "She offers us twigs to line our nests!" The other birds jeered.

"No, no! They're magical," Dotty pleaded. "Take them, please. They're yours."

Dotty gave the sticks a squeeze. What were they supposed to do anyway? "Pip, I really need you!" she muttered under her breath.

The chough moved his beak up and down, as if sniffing the air. Seemingly satisfied, he took a step back. "No magic that I can smell." His pointed red beak approximated a grin.

Dotty stood her ground. "I'll show you." She shook the sticks in her fist. Still nothing.

The assembly of birds inched towards her. "It seems ye have nothing to offer the brethren," the chough smirked. He hopped forward an inch.

"Wait!" Turning to one side, Dotty quietly dropped one of the sticks to the floor, petrified in case it should make the tiniest sound. But there was nothing. No Pip and no magic. What were they supposed to do anyway? Dotty couldn't believe it. In her haste to leave the Grateful Dragon she had clean forgotten to ask Pip what to do with them. "Oh work, you stupid things – work!"

"It looks like there be no-one here to save ye, little miss," the bird mocked. The others circled, closing in, their faces sharp, hungry.

Chapter 23

"Drat!" Dotty exclaimed, flinging the silly little bits of wood hard to the floor in her frustration.

Suddenly there was an almighty *boom* and a blinding green flash. Dotty stood rooted to the spot, whilst frightened birds squawked and fluttered as they scrabbled for safety in the cracks of the walls. But as quickly as the light had come, it was gone and Dotty once again found herself standing in the gloom, her eyes adjusting to the lengthening shadows and the birds that inhabited them.

Suddenly the chough was upon her, his beak inches from her face. "Is that all they gave ye?" He uttered a harsh cackle, his voice like gravel. "A firecracker? It'll take more'n that, m'dear, to put the brethren off their *supper.*"

Dotty felt the blood drain from her face in horror. All around her little beetle-y eyes glinted and small beaks clacked together in anticipation of a Dotty-flavoured snack, as one by one the birds began to close in. The little red-legged chough was the first to advance, taking two small hops forward he lunged towards her and gave her shin a sharp peck. Dotty screamed. Suddenly they were all upon her. Dotty threw herself to the ground, hands over her head, protecting her face. But as she did so, there was a second blinding flash and then a thud, followed by another, and another, and then a double thud that sounded like —could it be boots landing?

With one valiant effort Dotty flung out her arms, shooing the attacking birds away from her face so she could look. It was only then that Dotty saw the broken, ancient hearth that lay at the back of the room, shuddering and shaking as it spewed out set after set of black hobnailed boots. It was the sweeps! A dozen of them or more, it seemed like. The sticks must have sent out some kind of signal – like a distress flare from a battleship. Thank goodness for magick!

Dotty watched the tables turn swiftly as the birds shrieked and screamed, scattering to the four walls and rising up into the air as they tried to escape the blows of the sweeps' brooms. But still she stood trapped in the middle of them as she searched wildly about her looking for a way out. All of a sudden Pip seemed to appear from out of nowhere, and with a quick, "Come on!" he grabbed her by the arm and pulled her through the tangle of birds and bodies and out towards the moorland path and safety.

"Run!" Pip shouted. Dotty did not hesitate to follow.

As they streaked along the path Dotty glanced back, unsure whether anyone pursued them. But the way behind them was clear. She scanned what she could still make out of the castle ruin that had almost been the scene of her downfall. She just hoped she had done enough to persuade her treacherous ally to help them.

Chapter 24

An Eye for an Eye

The fairground was quiet now. It was after dark and everyone had gone home. Madam Orla's tent stood dark and quiet, no light escaping from within.

Mordecai and his two winged escorts, the ravens, landed near the tent.

"It's here, it's here," squawked Stoneye.

"Be there anyone at home?" asked Mordecai.

"It be fair dark inside," replied Stalefoot.

"Let us pay the crone a visit, shall we?" Mordecai advanced towards the tent.

The two ravens went in first, opening the tent flap a crack to look inside. Only the glowing embers from a small woodstove lit the blackness of the room, forcing the birds' eyes to make a further adjustment to the dim light. The crone was sitting in a corner, perfectly still in her chair. Next to her was a battered old table, littered with cards, amongst which lay a crystal ball.

"Come in, come in," cried Stoneye to his master outside.

"She sleeps, she sleeps," Stalefoot called.

Satisfied, Mordecai stepped into the tent, flinging aside the canvas flap so that a ray of moonlight shone into the room. The silver light lit up the woman's wrinkled face, to which was strapped Mordecai's mechanical eye. One of the ravens let out a squawk of recognition, but the other nudged him to be quiet.

It was the old woman who broke the silence first, addressing her intruders. "O-ho," she cackled, the mechanical eye that she wore strapped to her head zipping into focus. "I see you. But it seems you do not see me."

"No indeed, madam. I be blind as ye once were. I be Mordecai the Eyeless." He took a low bow. "I come as emissary for the Vagabond King. We have run into some trouble with the Fae and he wishes ye to provide him with another spell."

"He has upset them?" the woman asked. As she leaned forward the mechanical eye buzzed and whirred into focus, its red light flashing in the bird's great unseeing eyes.

Chapter 24

"Nay, madam. It appears that by your magic we released some Catchers into the woods."

"Indeed?"

"Aye, madam. The Faer folk be not happy. They consider them pests and wish to be rid of them. Know ye of a way to reverse their mischief?"

The fortune teller nodded wisely, the lens of the mechanical eye withdrawing with a short whirr as it settled back to rest.

After some time she spoke. "You will know, bird, that it is a magical fire through which they travelled?"

"Indeed, madam. It was I who entered the Fae through the fiery portal."

The crone nodded. "Then know this: the only fire that can lead them out is the fire that brought them in."

"But that fire is gone," Mordecai replied.

The old woman chuckled. "You are unversed in the ways of the Faer ones. Light a new fire from the embers of the old." She turned to a rickety old shelving unit that stood behind her and rummaged in amongst the bottles and potions that covered it.

After what seemed like quite some time, and with much clinking and clattering, she turned back to the trio, holding in her hand a small glass vial filled with dirty green liquid. "Take this," she said. "Pour it onto the fire when you are ready. It will recreate the portal and the Catchers will be drawn to it."

The old crone leaned forward, her breath hot and foul on Mordecai's face. "When all the Catchers are crowded around the portal, then - and only then - must you put out the fire. When you do this the portal will be destroyed, leaving the Catchers trapped as they were before, in between the land of the Fae and the world of men. And so they will become lost to you."

"But what if the fire is not put out quickly enough, or some of the Catchers escape? What happens then?"

"Then," the crone cackled wickedly, "you will once again be in need of the services of Madam Orla. And I will wish another favour from your master." She handed Mordecai the vial. "A touch of his youth, perhaps?"

Mordecai took the vial and tucked it under his wing. "Thank ye, madam." His henchmen drew in closer to the old woman. "And now that me master's business with ye be concluded, it appears I have some of me own to resolve."

For the first time in their presence the crone looked surprised. "And, pray tell, what is that, Mordecai the Eyeless?"

"Oh it be nothing really." He leaned closer, his sharp beak brushing the woman's face. "Just the small matter of an eye."

Chapter 25

Alliance

Dotty stood in the clearing next to the castle, watching the birds rebuild the fire through which Mordecai had first followed her into her vision. To her, the whole situation seemed a little surreal. Despite Mordecai's guarantee of safety, and the presence of Pip and the other sweeps in the woods, she still felt distinctly uncomfortable about the fragile alliance that existed between them and this gargantuan bird and his vicious army.

She eyed the birds with suspicion as they flitted and hopped about, bringing bits and pieces of twig and dried leaves and moss, and then larger sticks to the site of the fire, placing them on top of the cold ash left from the previous one. Dotty instantly recognised the small red-legged chough as he hobbled about uncomfortably. He looked like he had taken quite a beating in the fight with the sweeps. He flitted to and fro, one wing hanging low, a leg tucked awkwardly under him. He would not meet Dotty's gaze.

Finally, the fire was set and a sweep stepped forward and put a spark to it, the dry tinder going up almost immediately in the warm September air. Dotty watched the flames as they established themselves, rising and billowing in the breeze. The greener wood crackled and spat, causing a crow to squawk dramatically and scurry to the shadows, away from its leaping orange tongues. It was time.

Mordecai stepped forward, addressing Dotty. "It looks like we be set, missy."

Dotty nodded and moved aside, allowing Mordecai to step forward with a small glass vial in his claw, containing something dirty and green.

"Hang on a minute," Dotty felt suddenly panicky. "What about the Vagabond King? What if he shows up?"

"He knows nothing of this, missy, be assured," croaked Mordecai.

Pip interjected "Don't worry, miss. We sweeps are keeping him busy on…another matter."

"Okay," Dotty took a deep breath. "Then I guess we're ready."

Chapter 25

Very carefully, Mordecai emptied the contents of the vial into the fire and hopped back. The tinder started to smoke, and then as it cleared Dotty saw that the flames had turned from red and gold to green and blue, and she felt the heat from the blaze subside. The portal was open once more.

Dotty took a few more steps away from the fire, giving Mordecai room to manoeuvre. Lifting his feet up and away from the flames, the giant magpie soared upwards and then swooped down, diving through the shimmering mist that hung above it, in a single beat of his wings.

Alliance

Chapter 26

The New Bargain

Once through the portal, Mordecai alighted, waiting for his senses to clear. Almost at once everything felt heightened. Touch, smell, even the taste of the air all were rendered crystal clear in an instant. As before, his eyes took the longest to adjust, giving the feeling of coming out of a fog. His vision cleared gradually, first revealing dark shadows and then shades of grey, finally brightening and sharpening into a full spectrum of colour.

Clutching a package in his newly-mended claws, he began to move forwards through the forest he now well-recognised and towards the woodland glade beyond which he knew he would find his prize. He could feel the presence of the

Dream Catchers in the woods, always fractionally out of reach, just beyond his line of vision. They whispered and echoed, buzzing at the corners of his perception: a shadow here, a flicker there. They made him uneasy and it surprised him that he hadn't noticed them before; although, of course, until now his focus had always been on following the girl.

As he moved away from the portal Mordecai could sense the Catchers reaching past him and the air prickled with their curiosity. He turned, taking time to view the opening from the inside for the first time, and saw the camp fire that lay beyond. Green sparks flew high into the air, spitting and crackling as they rose up above the flames. And he saw the silhouettes of spirits moving around it. Behind him, closer to the fire, he felt a heightened sense of being, the whisperings of the Catchers moving out of the imagination and into the ordinary range of his hearing. He could almost see shapes moving in and out of the mist, dancing by the fire's edge.

But this was no time to be mesmerised by otherworldly distractions. He needed to press on and let the magick do its part, drawing the Catchers in whilst he worked. Turning once again into the forest he pressed on, his sleek black wings carrying him easily along, the ease of movement in his snow white wing feathers all at once bringing pleasure to his flight.

Chapter 26

It didn't take long to get to the glade, although all the while he had a sense of pushing against an ebbing tide, as the Wisps made their way towards the promise of the flames. It was only a short push beyond the glade to the tree with its strange and unnatural fruit. It was indeed an odd thing. The tree itself appeared dead: a skeleton or shell of something that once lived. Or perhaps it had never had life of its own. But the things that hung upon it all exuded a glow of life: each having its own individual light. Together, they made the tree seem alive with electricity, like a Christmas tree hung about with coloured fairy lights.

Mordecai took a furtive look around to check for the company of others, but he saw no one and sensed only the Catchers making their exit from the woods. Satisfied that he was otherwise alone, he scanned the assorted objects that hung upon the tree's branches: a pair of glasses, a ring, a pocket watch, and finally, a small oval locket: gold, set with emeralds and seed pearls on its surface. There it was: the source of all his recent troubles. He hesitated before seizing it, afraid that the light that glowed around it might burn or injure him. But it did not, and he unhooked the locket easily enough from its gnarled branches. Holding it safely in his beak, he studied the tree for a minute further. There were so many pretty, shiny objects adorning that tree.

Should he take one thing more? Something for his trouble?

"Would you steal back that which you have bargained away, Mordecai the Eyeless?" A cool voice came from beyond the tree. It was the hob.

Startled, Mordecai dropped the locket from his beak, and it fell to the ground with a thud. Then, composing himself, he gave his feathers a shake, placing one claw protectively over the locket as he did so. "Not steal: swap. I bring ye your gold in return." He threw the package to the ground. "I have spent none of it: it be untouched."

The hob appeared from behind the tree, the brilliance of its light hurting Mordecai's eyes and making him squint.

"But I have no need of it. If I had wanted gold I would not have traded it with you." The hob moved forward, his silvered limbs shimmering in the half light. "The things I value have no monetary worth." He motioned towards the strange tree. "They are things of rarity and magick: everyday objects imbued with singular powers. These things I can use better than any cache of treasure. Have you not heard the expression, 'all that glitters is not gold'?" The hob smiled coldly. "But of course you haven't, magpie."

"The locket is not for me. I wish to return it to its rightful owner: the girl."

Chapter 26

Suddenly the hob's light burned more fiercely, white hot with pure anger. "You would trespass on this hallowed place? You would steal from me to help a mortal girl? Tell me, bird, are you without your wits in the land of men, as well as your eyes?"

"I gave her me word is all." Mordecai argued defensively.

The hob laughed. "And you, Mordecai the Eyeless, are as good as your word, are you?"

"What has man or bird, if not his word?" he answered.

"If you think you can persuade me that the milk of human kindness motivates you: a bird, then you are more a fool than I thought when you traded me this trinket for a simple pot of gold." The faerie smiled a wicked little smile. "I suspect you owe the girl a debt."

Mordecai looked down, avoiding the creature's gaze. The hob chuckled.

"Nevertheless, I see you are a loyal creature. Now that is something of rare worth. Although the one who calls himself the Vagabond King might scarce agree."

"He betrayed me," replied the bird. "He be no longer deserving of me loyalty."

The hob paused a moment. "And what think you of me?" he asked. "Might *I* be deserving of such loyalty?"

"I cannot say. What might ye offer me in return for me service?"

The New Bargain

The hob picked up the locket from where it lay on the grass. He held it out and flashed a cunning smile. "What say you to a new bargain?"

Chapter 27

Catching the Catchers

Dotty watched through the portal that hovered above the blue-green flames like some strange and magical looking glass. Dotty thought it odd to see fire, but not to be able to feel it, for the magick took all the heat from it, although its flickering tongues still licked the night sky.

Until now, the vision of the forest that Dotty watched through the portal had felt peaceful and still. But as Dotty looked on, the air around it seemed to become agitated: disturbed by the clamour of spirits, impatient and curious. It was the Dream Catchers. They were trying to get free: to escape through the fabric of the portal and be released into the world to go in search of dreaming innocents from whom they could feed. Dotty felt momentarily panicked; but then reminded herself that they would not get their wish. For the magick prevented them, and all they could do was watch through the window and see the fire that lay beyond.

Mordecai seemed to have been an age and Dotty was growing impatient. But at last she saw him flitting through the trees, on a course that headed straight for the portal. His great wings were spread wide, his movement through the Fae purposeful, focused. As he neared the fire and the world of Men, Dotty nodded a signal to him from the other side: she was ready.

As Mordecai neared the portal entrance, he saw the waiting figure of the girl with wild, dark hair and determined eyes, signalling to him to act. He also saw the amorphous forms of the Dream Catchers clamouring at the opening. Suddenly he realised that he would not be able to cross over from the Fae back into the world of men without bringing at least some of the Catchers with him: as soon as he breached the portal, they would be freed. This meant his only hope of getting the locket back through the portal while keeping the Catchers at bay would be to toss the locket to the fire and hope that it could be retrieved before the flames destroyed it.

Chapter 27

But he had nothing to fear, he reminded himself. The portal no longer mattered to him, for he had struck a bargain with the hob.

His decision made, Mordecai hesitated, steeling himself to do this one final act. Then, after a moment, he returned Dotty's signal, nodding back that he was ready. Mordecai watched his brethren for a minute. In some small way he would miss them. But his mind was made up now. With a swift movement of his powerful curved beak, he hurled the locket as hard as he could, straight through the portal and into the flames.

Something in the bird's demeanour told Dotty that he was not planning to follow the locket through the portal. Vainly she shouted after him, "No!" and waved her arms desperately back and forth. "Don't do it. You must travel with the locket. Quick! Someone! We have to stop him."

The birds in the clearing started to leap and jump at the fire, shrieking "Master! Do not leave us." But the sweeps held them back from the flames.

As the body of the locket tore out of the Fae and into the world of men the Catchers dived after it, trying to steal through the break in the portal's seal. But instead they sealed their own fate. For as the locket passed through the portal, Dotty threw a bucket of water on the fire, dousing the flames in an instant.

Dotty watched on. There was a rush of air and smoke rising upwards, and a sound that seemed to Dotty like something that lingered between a breath and a scream. It was the Catchers' recognition, perhaps, that they were trapped hopelessly between the magical land of the Fae and the world of men. And then suddenly the portal was gone, as quick as the blink of an eye; leaving behind it barely a pinprick of light that was fast extinguished.

Was that really it? Dotty thought it seemed almost too easy.

On the other side of the veil the great bird, Mordecai, stood for a moment, listening intently to the sound of the forest around him. Then, satisfied that the whisperings of the Catchers were gone, he stretched out his beautiful sleek wings and made his way back into the woodland realm of the Fae.

After a short time he alighted in the glade where the hob's strange tree glowed blue in the half-light. Taking advantage of his newly-restored sight, he searched for a moment, seeking something among the branches. The item found, he gave a satisfied nod and took off into the forest.

There was indeed something hanging in the tree that had not been there before. It was an odd-looking item made of metal and glass, with thick leather straps: something which no longer held any value for the bird who had once been known as Mordecai the Eyeless. But it felt good for him to see it there, a reminder of his former life.

Of course anyone who knew Mordecai would have recognised it straight away. It was the great bird's mechanical eye.

Catching the Catchers

Chapter 28

The Carrion Curse

With the fire now out and the portal closed Dotty, armed with an oven glove stolen from Gobby's kitchen, wasted no time in quickly reaching into the blackened embers of the fire to fish out the gold trinket that Mordecai had thrown there. Water had mixed with ash and created a thick black mud that covered its surface. But even dirty as it was, Dotty could see that this was her mother's locket. Finally: Dotty was reunited with the Calendar House Key.

It was all she could do not to hug the thing to her chest, but Dotty was blessed with common sense and, even after a few seconds in the flame, she knew it could be hot. So instead she quickly dumped it into the bucket that had held the water used to douse the fire. There was only a small puddle of water remaining at the bottom, but it was sufficient to both clean and cool the locket so that finally she could touch it. This done, she fished it out of the water and placed the chain quickly around her neck, tucking the locket safely down the front of her jumper.

Her task over, Dotty became aware of the cacophony of sound that had erupted around her, as the sweeps cheered in celebration.

Pip stepped forward and saluted her. "Hoorah for Dotty!"

"Three cheers for the keeper of the Calendar House Key," the others cried. "Tonight we will celebrate. Call the Council for a sweeps' feast!"

But equally loud were the mournful screechings and wailings from the birds that filled the clearing.

"Master? Where be our Master? Shall he not return?"

"He is trapped! Trapped with the fairies and the spirits. This be sweeps' work. They did this to us!"

"Nay." The tattered, sorrowful chough turned to Dotty, pointing his one good wing towards her. "Ye did this." His voice was full of menace.

"No," Dotty countered. "It was Mordecai's idea, his choice."

Chapter 28

"The Carrion Curse!" a great raven shouted from behind her.

"Yes, the Carrion Curse," chorused others.

"Pip, what's the Carrion Curse?" Dotty asked, feeling slightly panicked.

"Let's just say I think we'd better go." Pip quickly steered them both around the gathering birds.

They fought their way through the crowd, tripping over jays and jackdaws as they swarmed at their feet.

"Fancy a bit of light chimney hopping, miss?" Pip grinned, ducking a swooping starling.

"Do I ever!"

As the sweeps made a bid to close in on the angry gathering and keep them at bay, Dotty and Pip made a dash for it, steering over, under, and around birds that seemed to come from every corner of earth and sky. The castle ruin was only a few short steps away.

Dotty was scared to enter it again, given that she had nearly been eaten by a murder of angry crows, last time she was there. She knew it contained their best, and possibly only, route of escape, though, so they pushed on.

As they ran, the chanting of the birds grew louder, their squawks and cackles forming a vile curse that filled the air and echoed on the stones of the ancient ruin.

"Dorothea nevermore,
Key-keeper nevermore,
Thou that takes our Master from us,
Nevermore, nevermore."

The birds shrieked and bayed, drumming their feet on the forest floor, bashing at the stones with their wingtips.

Dotty could see the fireplace at the far end of the roofless room. "Quick!" she wailed to Pip.

"Almost there," he replied, half-pushing, half-carrying her in his haste to get to the broken hearth.

"Clear skies, nevermore,
Restful slumber, nevermore,
Curse that never shall peace find you,
Dorothea nevermore."

Dotty and Pip stepped into the empty fireplace. "Home?" he asked.

Dotty clutched her mother's locket tightly in her hand. "No," she said. "To the hospital."

"Right you are," said Pip, and raising his broom aloft, he put an arm around her waist and they lifted up and off into the night.

Chapter 29

Awake

A student nurse sat herself down wearily in an armchair, putting her feet up on the low table and taking a long slurp of her tea. There was no one else there that night, as all the other girls were still on shift.

The armchair was threadbare and the table ringed and scratched but, after a 14-hour shift at the hospital, the student's common room was nothing less than heaven on earth to her. She kicked off her hospital shoes, stretching her aching stockinged feet, and took a bite of a Twix bar. Bliss. She had neither the inclination nor the wherewithal to cook tonight.

Shifting a little in her chair, the nurse had half a mind to sleep where she sat, so tired was she. But she knew it would be better to take weary limbs off to bed than to wake up with a crick in the neck. She took another sip of her tea and settled herself into the chair. Then, closing her eyes for just a moment, she drifted off.

The nurse awoke with a start at the sound of a rumbling in the fireplace. The chimney breast vibrated a little, shaking the picture off the wall, which landed with a smash on the tiled hearth. She jumped out of her seat in alarm. She had never noticed a train line nearby that might cause such rumblings. But then she was always so tired. Or perhaps it was a low-flying aircraft.

Mug still in hand, she took a step towards the kitchen to fetch the dust pan. The rumbling increased, and then all of a sudden, like the popping of a cork out of champagne, two pairs of feet appeared on the fireside rug, quickly followed by their owners: a small boy of about 13, clutching what appeared to be a sweep's broom, and with him a slightly younger girl wearing an oversized woolly jumper.

The nurse screamed.

The boy doffed his cap. "Evening, miss."

Following a hasty exit from the nurse's common room, Dotty and Pip raced along the hospital corridor. Dotty directed a scowl at Pip as they fled. "Really?"

"Honestly, miss, it was the best I could do." He thrust his hands into his pockets. "Anyways, you said you wanted to go to the hospital."

"Yes, the hospital, not the nurses' lodgings! You frightened that poor girl half to death." They took a right turn.

"Well, there aren't any fireplaces in the hospital: 'cept for the furnace, and I didn't fancy that – did you? As I said, it was the best I could do."

Dotty harrumphed. "I suppose the Council will have something to say about it, too, will they?"

Pip shrugged. "I'm sure they'll forgive me. Look, isn't that the ward up ahead?"

They advanced more steadily now their goal was in sight. Dotty hated the hospital. Everything was cold, hard, sanitised. And on the ward itself, a deathly silence reigned. No amount of chocolates or teddies could erase the heartbreak of the worried parents, aunts, and grandparents that held vigil at the sleeping girls' bedsides.

But as they neared the door of the ward, all was not silence. In fact it was quite the opposite. Everywhere was chaos. The central station was buzzing, doctors and nurses running hither and thither. Dotty's stomach did a nervous flip. Please let everything be okay.

Then Dotty saw Sylv's dad – well, the back of his head, anyway. As she rushed forwards he turned and Dotty saw that he was grinning from ear to ear, as was the girl that sat in the hospital bed behind him. It was Sylv.

"Sylv, you're awake!"

For once without words, Sylv beamed and drew Dotty to her.

"They're all awake, Dot," Sylv's dad said, grabbing both girls together and hugging them tight. "Thank my stars, they're all okay."

Pip watched on at the doorway for a moment. And then, satisfied that his charge was safe, he slipped quietly away.

Chapter 30

An Unhappy Twist

For the first time in what seemed like forever Dotty went to bed that night without being fearful that she might wake within a forest vision. And her instincts were correct: for she was not roused from sleep by the sound of Sarah calling her name, or prodding her silently awake with a cold, hard finger. What woke her was an unnatural light: a pale blue light that started as a pinprick in the darkness of her bedroom and grew ever bigger and brighter until finally her mind told her to wake up.

The eerie glow that pervaded the room might not have bothered Dotty if she had closed the curtains to her four-poster bed, but she had been so tired that she had neglected to do so. Yawning, she raised herself up onto her elbows and rubbed the sleep from her eyes. What was that? And then it dawned upon her. This was faerie light.

Dotty sat up fully and braced herself, expecting a visit from the hob. Whatever could he want? Not to claim the Calendar House Key again, surely?

But it was no hob that emerged from the blue. Dotty watched as the glow expanded further, and she could just make out the forest of the Fae undulating at the centre of her vision.

Then, without warning, like an ugly blue mouth, the strange phenomenon spat something, or rather someone, out onto her floor. And in an instant the light reduced back to nothing more than a spark that quickly extinguished, leaving a tattered, broken form lying on Dotty's carpet. It was as if some kind of hellish giant cat had left Dotty an unsavoury present on the rug.

For a moment Dotty's tired brain couldn't work out what it was that had been ejected from the Fae in such an abrupt fashion. Was it Mordecai? But then the bundle gave a small, weak cough. Dotty sprang from the bed, the full horror of what she was seeing dawning upon her. "Sarah. Whatever happened? Are you all right?" Dotty couldn't believe it was her. Had the hob released her? Surely not?

But wait a moment. This was not the Sarah of Dotty's visions. This was the tiny, broken dying girl that she had sent into the Fae in place of Joe. Oh no – this could not be. This was simply terrible - horrifying: wicked.

Sinking to the floor, Dotty tried to pick Sarah up: to hold Sarah in her arms, to comfort her. "It'll be okay. Don't worry. Just hang on."

The little girl smiled weakly. "Dotty," she whispered, "I am punished." And then her body fell limp.

"No! Sarah, wake up." Dotty screamed in anguish. "Somebody help me. Please." Frantic, Dotty pressed her fingers against Sarah's tiny, fragile wrist, trying to find a pulse. But she didn't really know how to do it – only what she had seen on the television – and she felt nothing.

"Help!" Dotty cried again. In desperation, she stared hard at the small girl's chest, desperately seeking even the smallest rise and fall in it. She put her cheek to Sarah's face, trying to feel if there was any hint of a breath. But there was nothing. Sarah was dead.

Great-Uncle Winchester was first on the scene. He quickly alerted the Sweep's Council, who wasted no time in sending a couple of emissaries from the sweep world to claim the child's body. Somehow the sight of two burly sweeps carrying poor Sarah away made the death seem all the more tragic. Her lifeless body was so frail that a single man could have picked her up as easily as lifting an injured bird back up to its nest. If only Sarah could have been saved so easily.

Dotty fought to speak through tears. "Why?" was just about the best she could manage.

"I think," said Great-Uncle Winchester, "we must assume that she was expelled from the Fae by the hob as punishment for leading you to the Calendar House Key." He shook his head sadly. "But it seems to me a sore punishment for a crime committed by such an innocent."

Dotty felt a twinge of guilt, followed quickly by anger. "He killed her!"

"In our eyes, perhaps," Dotty's great-uncle replied, gently. "But in the eyes of the hob, he simply returned her to her earthly state: the same state in which he found her with us and from which he took her. Sad to say, but the poor child was dying and we knew it."

"But it's not fair," Dotty argued. "She didn't deserve to die. How could he save her and then turn around and 'un-save' her, just because she contacted a friend? It seems so heartless and cruel to punish her like that." Dotty sobbed. "We've got the Calendar House Key back, but at what price? It can't ever be worth a life, surely."

"I know, dear girl. I know." Great-Uncle Winchester gave her a long hug. "And you're right. The whole thing really isn't fair at all."

Chapter 31

Normality (of sorts)

The month of December came and went and both home and school had settled back into normality, of a sort. And so it was that, at 6.45 a.m on a cold January morning, Dotty found herself up and dressed in a freshly pressed school uniform, ready to start a new term at school. Alone, Dotty dragged the heavy trunk down the corridor, and then bumped it drearily down the stairs. Gobby had told her that Mr. Strake would bring it down, but he was late and she would miss the bus if she didn't get a move on.

In truth, part of her wanted to miss the bus. Going back to school wasn't exactly top of her list of priorities right now. She was rather too busy trying to absorb the events of the last couple of months to be bothered about that. But she knew that being late back would just add oil to the fire, so she figured she was best getting it over and done with.

She puffed a little as she lugged the case down the last of the stairs. It really was too heavy for her to handle on her own. On reaching the bottom step a solution occurred to her, however. The floors of the back corridor were wooden and highly-polished. Except for a couple of rugs, if she got some momentum going she could skate it along quite nicely. Shame she had grown out of her roller blades. Still, her birthday was coming up – she could ask for a new pair.

With a couple of large shoves the trunk glided quite nicely, polished leather against the polished floors (good old Gobby and her marvellous housekeeping skills), and Dotty began to pick up pace. Before long she was hurtling along the passage at what any adult would have called quite an alarming pace. What Dotty hadn't thought about was what might happen when she actually hit carpet.

The first such carpet sat between Strake's and Great-Uncle Winchester's study doors. Making a split-second decision, Dotty decided that if she gave the trunk an extra boost at just the right moment, it would mount the rug, hopefully not getting caught on the fringe, and keep on going. She miscalculated. The heavy leather case hit the edge of the rug at a hair-raising speed and the carpet rucked up, taking the case with it and tipping it momentarily up on its end. It came crashing back down onto the now somewhat-displaced carpet, springing open as it went and spewing its contents all over the hall floor.

"Darn it!" Dotty looked at the mess in dismay. This was the last thing she needed. As quickly as she could, she started to gather up armfuls of clothes, books, and toiletries and bung them at top speed back into the trunk.

In her haste, her foot slipped on the shiny floorboards and she went skidding into the wall, the blow to her shoulder as it hit the wall being only slightly softened by the fabric of the tapestry that hung from it. As her shoulder hit home, her foot also made contact, kicking something from out of place behind the tapestry that skidded across the floor. It was Great-Uncle Winchester's photo album! With everything going on she had completely forgotten that she and Sylv had hidden it there after discovering it hidden in the family vault.

"What on earth are you doing, Miss Parsons?" Strake loomed over her. Clearly all the kerfuffle had brought him out of his office.

Quickly Dotty crouched to the floor, squirrelling the album away under a stray blouse. "I dropped my trunk," she answered defensively, continuing to scoop up armfuls of her possessions and dump them in the case.

"I see." He looked as if he had swallowed a wasp. "I had understood from Mrs. Gobbins that I was to bring that down for you. I was just on my way."

"Sure you were," Dotty muttered under her breath.

"Well, you can take it to the bus for me," she replied, putting the last blouse on top and slamming the lid shut. The sound of wheels grating on the gravel came from outside the front door. "It's here now."

"Of course, Miss Parsons." Strake offered her a weasel-y smile, his bony, long-fingered hands closing around the thick leather handles.

Ugh! He gave her the creeps.

Dotty didn't tell her great-uncle's personal secretary goodbye; nor did he expect such a nicety, for he turned his back on her and slunk back into the house just as soon as her case was safely deposited in the bus's ample luggage hold. As the driver pulled out over the gravel, Dotty did allow herself to look out of the back window though, and give the Calendar House a little wave farewell.

Then settling down into her seat, she opened the paper parcel given to her by Gobby as a parting gift, and as she tucked into a still-warm sticky sweet Queen of Hearts biscuit, allowed herself a little smile.

Stumbling (quite literally) across the photo album had been quite the piece of last-minute luck. At long last she had something real to show for her genealogy project, and she decided to take it as a sign: perhaps going back to school wasn't going to go so badly after all.

From Mrs Gobbins' Kitchen

Welsh Cakes for Breakfast

"It was 7.15 a.m. Dotty pulled open the heavy bedroom drapes and looked out into the eerie morning light. For a brief moment she watched the first mist rising from the moor in the distance. Then tripping down the back steps and in to the kitchen, she found Gobby already busying herself, merrily humming some unrecognisable tune.

Dotty's eyes came at once to rest on a rather precarious but wonderfully scented pile of freshly baked Welsh cakes, still steaming on the hot plate. Grabbing a couple, Dotty pocketed one and shoved the other unceremoniously into her mouth, whilst simultaneously making a quick dash towards the kitchen door. There was a lot to do before eleven o'clock and her first meeting with Great-Uncle Winchester.

"My! Aren't you in a hurry this morning," remarked Gobby, cheerily. "I hope you like the Welsh cakes." She eyed the crummy evidence peeking out of Dotty's jumper pocket. "I made them especially. I thought they might remind you of home. I expect your mother cooked them all the time, did she?" The old cook smiled benignly.

Dotty didn't like to say they almost never ate Welsh cakes in her household; and those that they did eat certainly weren't home made by her mum. They were more likely to be bought from the local Tesco's or from Eddie's on the corner. But Dotty appreciated the sentiment anyway."

About traditional Welsh Cakes

Welsh cakes, also known as *pics*, or *bakestones* - after the cast iron griddle they are traditionally cooked in, have been popular in Wales since the late 1800s. Welsh cakes are small, round flat cakes – a little like drop scones - made with currants and mixed spice.

Welsh cakes taste best when served warm sprinkled with sugar, but they can be eaten cold, too. Unlike traditional English scones, they are usually eaten without the accompaniment of jam or butter (although see below for Mrs Gobbins' festive recipe twist).

You will need:

- 225g/8oz/1 cup plain (all purpose) flour
- 100g/4oz/ ½ cup butter (salted or unsalted)
- 75g/3oz/1/3 cup caster (superfine) sugar[2]
- 50g/2oz/¼ cup currants
- ½ teaspoon (tsp) baking powder[3]
- ¼ tsp mixed spice[4]
- 1 egg
- A pinch of salt
- A little milk to bind

---

[2] If you don't have caster or superfine sugar, you can use an electric coffee grinder or blender to grind your granulated sugar down to a finer consistency.

[3] Baking powder is a raising agent commonly used in British baking. You can make a substitute baking powder by mixing 1 tsp of baking soda with ½ tsp cornstarch and ½ tsp cream of tartar.

[4] A mix of spices often used in traditional British baking. A rough and ready substitute in the US is pumpkin pie spice, or you can make your own by mixing 4 tsp cinnamon, 2 tsp coriander, 1 tsp allspice, ½ tsp nutmeg, ½ tsp ginger and ¼ tsp cloves.

What to do:

Sift the flour, baking powder and mixed spice together into a mixing bowl.

Cut up the butter and rub into the flour.

Stir in the sugar and currants, pour in the egg and mix to form a dough. Use a little milk if the mixture is dry.

Roll the dough out on a lightly floured surface to about the thickness of a biscuit. Use a pastry cutter to cut out rounds. They should be roughly circular, a few inches (7–8 cm) in diameter and about half an inch (1–1.5 cm) thick.

Cook the cakes on a greased bake stone, griddle or simply in the frying pan, until golden. The heat should not be too high, as the cakes will cook on the outside too quickly, and not in the middle. Once cooked, sprinkle with caster sugar and serve.

For a seasonal alternative Mrs Gobbins suggests substituting the currants for mixed dried fruit and some grated orange rind. This festive version is delicious served with some softened butter combined with a little orange juice, zest and icing sugar.

Apple dragons!
Welsh cakes with grated apple added to the mix make for a tasty alternative to traditional Welsh Cakes, and they will stay moist in the tin for longer. The Welsh call these 'apple dragons'.

ABOUT THE AUTHOR

Emma Warner-Reed is a qualified lawyer, academic, legal journalist and author. Emma lives in a rural setting on the edge of the Yorkshire Dales with her husband, four small children and a plethora of animals, some of whom are more domesticated than others!

To date the first book in the series, DOTTY and the Calendar House Key, released in 2015, has received significant acclaim including the Literary Classics Silver Award for children's fantasy fiction, an exclusively five star rating on Amazon, the official Seal of Approval from Literary Classics and Honourable Mentions at the Los Angeles, New York, Amsterdam and Paris Book Festival Awards.

The second novel in The DOTTY Series, DOTTY and the Chimney Thief, has also recently been awarded gold by Literary Classics in the preteen mystery/thriller category.

DOTTY and the Dream Catchers is the third novel in The DOTTY Series. Look out for Dotty's fourth adventure, DOTTY and the Mermaid's Purse, coming soon!

Please feel free to contact Emma for interviews, quotes or comments about her writing via any of the methods listed on the contact page on the website. For regular news, reviews and updates on The DOTTY Series, subscribe to the DOTTY mailing list at www.thedottyseries.com, or follow Emma on Twitter or Facebook.

ACKNOWLEDGMENTS

Thank you, as ever, to my lovely little family for supporting me through the writing process, and to my literary colleagues who have inspired and encouraged me along the way.

In particular I would like to thank Team DOTTY, namely: Nancy Butts, Tara Brown, Rose English, Susan Jackson, Sophie Wallace, Alex Vere, Patrick, Belinda and Megan Brown, Louise Styan, Jane, Connor and Kara Johnson and Paul Douglas Lovell.

But most importantly thank you to everyone who has bought and read the first and second books in the DOTTY series and who have spurred me on to writing the third. A writer is nothing without their audience and so to you I offer my sincerest gratitude. Thank you for securing DOTTY's place in the literary world. I hope she and her friends continue to entertain you and many more people in the future.

34813485R00129

Printed in Great Britain
by Amazon